Peter Murphy is a senior writer for Dublin's *Hot Press*, and has contributed to *Rolling Stone* and *Music Week*. He is also a regular guest on RTE's arts show *The View*.

JOHN THE REVELATOR

John Devine is an introverted, watchful, adolescent boy. He's stuck in a small town, worried over by his single mother — the chain-smoking, bible-quoting Lily — and the gregarious but sinister Mrs Nagle. He yearns for escape. When the charismatic Jamey Corboy arrives in town, John's life suddenly fills with possibilities — welcome and otherwise — and as he hides from the reality of his mother's ever-worsening health, he is faced with a terrible dilemma.

PETER MURPHY

JOHN THE REVELATOR

Complete and Unabridged

ULVERSCROFT
Leicester

First published in Great Britain in 2009 by
Faber and Faber Limited
London

First Large Print Edition
published 2009
by arrangement with
Faber and Faber Limited
London

British Library CIP Data

Murphy, Peter, *1968 –*
John the revelator
1. Mothers and sons- -Fiction. 2. Single mothers- -
Fiction. 3. Adolescence- -Fiction. 4. Black humor.
5. Large type books.
I. Title
823.9'2–dc22

ISBN 978–1–84782–860–6

Published by
F. A. Thorpe (Publishing)
Anstey, Leicestershire
Set by Words & Graphics Ltd.
Anstey, Leicestershire
Printed and bound in Great Britain by
T. J. International Ltd., Padstow, Cornwall

This book is printed on acid-free paper

For Peadar and Betty

'And I John saw these things, and heard them.'

Revelation 22:8

1

I was born in a storm. My mother said the thunder was so loud she flinched when it struck, strobes of lightning and slam-dancing winds and volleys of rain for hours until it blew itself out and sloped off like a spent beast.

'I knew you were a boy,' she said. 'Heartburn. Sure sign of a man in your life.'

My name is John Devine. I was christened after the beloved disciple, the brother of James the Great. Our Lord called them the sons of thunder.

'John was Jesus' favourite,' my mother told me. 'The patron saint of printers and tanners and typesetters.'

When she got started on this, it could go on for hours. We were out walking the fields at the back of our house. I was still in short trousers. My mother strode ahead, hell bent on where she was going, and I had to trot to keep up.

'He was the only one to stay awake in the garden while Our Lord sweated blood,' she said. 'After the crucifixion, the emperor brought him to Rome to be flogged and beaten and thrown in a cauldron of boiling oil. They tried to poison him with wine, but the poison rose to the surface in the shape of a snake. In the end they banished him to Patmos, where he wrote the Book of Revelation.'

She took out her handkerchief and dribbled on it.

'The only apostle to escape martyrdom.'

And she wiped my face. The smell was like when you lick yourself, a compound of saliva and tissue and skin. I tried to pull away, but she wouldn't let go until she was satisfied I was clean.

'He died in the year a hundred and one. People believed that once a year his grave gave off a smell that could heal the sick. Just before John passed away, his followers carried him into the assembly at the church of Ephesus and asked him how to live. You know what he said?'

She stuffed the tissue up her sleeve.

'Little children, love one another.'

'That's all?'

'It's enough to be going on with.'

Said my mother, I was still an infant when we moved from the caravan near Ballo strand to a house a couple of miles outside Kilcody. Her mother and father willed it to her when they died. It was always so cold there you could see your breath hang in the air. Vines of ivy crawled across the pebble-dashed walls; weeds strangled the few sticks of rhubarb. There was a sandpit out the back, broken toys and mustard minarets of turd, an orange clothesline dripping laundry.

Every day after school I dragged my schoolbag home like it was a younger brother, let myself into the house and snapped on all the downstairs lights. There was a cactus on our kitchen windowsill, swollen green fingers and prickly white spines. Beside that was Haircut Charlie, the clown's head for planting seeds in, grass growing out of the tiny holes in his skull. A sacred-heart lamp glowed atop the mantelpiece. The floor was new blue linoleum with black patterns. One time a pipe under the sink leaked and we had to tear up the old stuff and underneath was crawling with bulbous pea-green slugs and brown fungus, like deformed bonsai trees.

My mother was still at work when I got home. She cleaned people's houses, and sometimes she took in clothes to be washed or mended. She said you could tell a lot about a person from their dirty laundry.

I'd sit over my homework at the kitchen table, anticipating the squeak of the gate, the parched bark of her cough. If she were late I'd start to worry that she'd been taken, and

I'd be sent to an orphanage or made to live with her friend Mrs Nagle or someone else old. But she always came home, shrugging out of her coat and saying she was choking for a cup of tea and a fag.

After the kettle went on she set the fire, placing bits of Zip under the briquettes, blue and orange flames licking at her fingers. Then she hefted the big pot onto the cooker.

'What's for dinner?'

'Pig's feet and hairy buttermilk.'

She spread the tablecloth and set the Delph. There were Polish cartoons on television, followed by the Angelus' boring bongs. My mother looked out the window and smoked while I ate. Her green eyes went grey whenever it rained and her hair was braided halfway down her back. After the washing up, she sat by the fire and read her Westerns. Gusts sobbed in the chimney and the fire spat and crackled.

'Book any good?'

'Ah — '

She slapped it shut, shook a Major's from the box and broke the filter off.

'Too many descriptions. I know what a tree looks like.'

The long nights were hard going. There was nothing to do but stare at the fire or listen to the wind howl around the eaves. The

4

sound reminded my mother of the night I was born.

'You were a typical boy,' she muttered under her breath. 'You came early.'

She screwed the truncated cigarette into a holder, lit it, took a deep breath and hawed a coil of smoke rings.

'It was about the thirty-fourth week.'

Then she leaned down and cranked the bellows, sending firefly flurries up the chimney. The fire blazed and crackled. She let me climb onto her lap, and her long fingers latticed across my stomach.

'There was a storm waiting to happen. The air was full of it.'

Her voice was deep and hypnotic, her breath warm against my crown. I closed my eyes and could almost smell the bonfire smoke as it drifted through the halting site, could see children running around with no trousers on, dogs tearing plastic bags of rubbish asunder. Air pressure like a migraine, pitchfork lightning and growls of thunder.

My mother described how when the storm struck she covered all the mirrors and crawled under her quilt and spread her hands over the swell of her belly, as though to protect me from the flashes of light and the noise. Fear churned her insides, travelled downward and became a clenching of pelvic muscles. She prayed it was a false alarm, tried to will the pangs away, but they intensified.

Her waters broke, soaking her leggings. She grabbed the bag she'd packed and out she went into the furious night and knocked on caravan windows. Nobody answered. Fear came upon her in great black waves. Panic welled up in her chest. But just as she despaired of finding help, a man appeared, unsteady and reeking of stout and sweat, but a man all the same, and he said he'd oblige her with a lift.

He was so jarred it took his Fiat three goes to exit the roundabout. Raindrops burst like pods against the windshield and water coated the road in a gleaming slick. My mother screwed her eyes shut and tried not to vomit or pass out as the waves of pain broke inside her lower parts.

They barely made it. A nurse helped my mother onto a trolley and wheeled her into the elevator cage and up to the delivery ward, no time for an epidural or any of that, just gas and air, my mother gumming on the apparatus like a suckling calf, hair plastered across her forehead, grinning at the midwife.

'You wouldn't happen to have a Baby Powers in your bag of tricks there,' she slurred.

'Be quiet and keep pushing,' said the midwife.

Breathing and pushing and moaning, gas and air and more breathing and pushing and moaning, and then I slithered out. The midwife scooped me up and the obstetrician cut the cord.

'A boy?' my mother asked, lifting her sweaty head.

'Aye,' said the midwife, as she wrapped me in a terry-towel.

'Any extras? Harelip? Flippers?'

'Whisht,' said the midwife.

The obstetrician looked me over, pronounced me hardy as a foal.

'He used to kick like one,' said my mother, and sank back into the pillows.

The recovery ward was full of night-gowned, slippered women, their faces flushed with fatigue. The rooms were warm and stuffy and my mother couldn't sleep. Soon as she could walk she called a taxi and took us home to the caravan. She padded the top drawer of an old teak dresser with blankets for a bassinet and placed me in it. Then the trouble started.

'You were a holy terror,' she said, mashing her fag into the seashell at her feet. 'You got in a knot with the colic and wouldn't let me sleep a wink. No sooner fed than you had to be winded. Then you'd poss up, and you'd be hungry again, so I'd feed you a second time, and as soon as I'd put you down to sleep you'd dirty your nappy, so I'd have to take you back up, and you'd be wide awake and hungry all over again. You had me vexed, son.'

For weeks she didn't get to finish a cup of tea or sit down to a proper meal. She barely spoke, and when she did it was through a veil of exhaustion, with a two-second satellite delay. Bad thoughts came. Fear for this tiny thing in her care, all kinds of wicked shadows snarling and pawing at the door. Some nights her moods got so moribund she harboured thoughts of putting a pillow over my head so as to get it over with quick.

'What stopped you?'

'You weren't baptised yet.'

Night after night I wailed my beetroot head off, and my mother walked the floor and patted my back in time with the songs playing on the local radio station, her walking, me bawling. One night, maybe three or four in the morning, the news came on. The man reading the headlines said the Met Office had issued a storm warning: gale-force winds, possible flooding. People were advised to stop home except for emergencies.

I went on caterwauling, and my mother rocked me in the crook of her shoulder, breathing my newborn smell. She held me to her breast and murmured into my pink cockleshell ear, 'It's an ill wind, son.'

And for no other reason than to drown out my squalling, she began to sing, the first thing that came into her head. As soon as I heard that sound, I fell silent. The song died in her mouth and she stared, stunned, as my eyelids came down and my body went limp. She laid me in my crib, checked my breath with her compact.

'At last,' she sighed, and crawled into bed.

It was the queerest thing, said my mother, but ever after that, I slept peacefully, ten hours a night. Provided she sang.

And I believed her, because a mother's word is gospel to her son.

Sundays we put on our good clothes and walked two miles to Mass in the village, a starched shirt collar gnawing into the back of my neck, my mother's perfume more potent than any incense. Father Quinn droned the First Letter of St Paul to the Corinthians like a dozy circuit-court judge, and I was bored stupid from listening to desultory hymns, the Eucharistic prayer, the mutters of people receiving Communion. The old ones took the

Eucharist on their tongue, the young ones in their palms.

'Body of Christ.'

'Amen.'

More hymn-singing. An early haemorrhage of dossers. The blessing.

'Mass is ended. Go in peace.'

My mother sighed.

'Thanks be to God.'

Every Sunday night after bath time I'd bend over and touch my toes while my mother shone a torch up my scut. The blood-rush made my head swim.

'What you looking for?' I said.

She was sat on the floor, a fag burning in the seashell ashtray beside her. I was about yea big.

'Worms.'

'How do worms get up my scut?'

'They don't.' Her voice was faint, distracted. 'They go in your mouth.'

She cleared her throat.

'*Steer clear of swine and creeping things and eaters of carrion and fish that have neither fins nor scales. These are unclean and harbour abominations in their flesh.* Leviticus, something-something.'

She switched off the torch and tapped my backside with it, the signal for me to pull up my pyjama bottoms.

'Do people die from worms?'

'It's been known to happen.'

She ran her fingernail along the teeth of a fine-toothed comb. It made a sound like Chinese music.

'But Our Lord said it's not what goes in your mouth that does the damage.'

She began to scour my hair for hoppers.

'It's what comes out.'

I plagued my mother with so many questions about worms she banned the subject. But one day she came home with a book — *Harper's Compendium of Bizarre Nature Facts* — containing loads of facts and figures about lizards and squids and duck-billed platypuses, and a whole chapter on worms entitled 'The Secret Life of Parasites'. The illustrated plates made my scalp tingle, like the time my head got ringworm. Mrs Nagle told me that ringworm is not actually a worm; it's a fungal infection. The medical name for it is dermatophytosis. You can get it on your body, your groin, your feet, your nails, even your beard. The kind I got was called *Tinea capitis*.

My mother started in on dinner and asked me to read aloud from the book, said the big words were good practice for school. I flipped straight to the part where it explained that a parasite is an organism that lives on or in another organism, known as the host. Big parasites can grow to dozens of feet in length. Some of the little ones are so tiny you can only see them under a microscope. Some parasites lay eggs; others duplicate themselves like bacteria.

Hunched over the sink, my mother unwrapped grease paper from around a gutted fish. I continued reading.

In ancient Asia and Africa, the book said, the cure for guinea worms was to lie down for a day, or two days, or a week, as long as it took, and slowly wind the worm around a stick to get it out alive. If you jerked it out, it'd break in half and die, infecting your insides. This is where the symbol for medicine comes from, two serpents wound around a staff, the *Caduceus*. In the Bible, serpents plagued the Israelites, but some people thought that was a poetic way of saying they had worms. In Edwardian times, they laid out the infirm and the consumptive in a room alongside troughs of flesh-fed maggots, believing the smell of ammonia and methane to have healing properties. They called this room the Maggotorium.

'That's the smell that came off St John's grave and healed people,' I said.

Peeling spuds, my mother grunted. I read on.

According to Harper, a nineteenth-century doctor called Friedrich Kuchenmeister tried to demonstrate the evolution of the bladder-worm into the tapeworm by feeding infected blood sausage to a convicted murderer four months before the man's execution. After the convict was put to death, they cut him open and found five-foot tapeworms in his stomach.

Eyes squeezed tight, my mother removed a slug from the heart of a cabbage and dropped it into the pedal bin. She plucked the cigarette from her mouth and looked at it.

'You know,' she said, squinting through fag-smoke, 'people say what doesn't kill you makes you stronger. Don't believe a word of it. What doesn't kill you just makes you sick. And what makes you sick — '

She ran a tap over her cigarette. It sizzled out.

' — Kills you.'

One school day Guard Canavan came to the Presentation Convent to tell us what happens to bad children when they die. He was a big tree-trunk of a man, dressed all in the same shade of navy blue, a voice so deep you felt rather than heard it.

'Do you know where bad boys and girls go, boys and girls?' he said.

No one answered except for Danny Doran, who put his hand up and said, 'England?'

Guard Canavan shook his head.

'No, but you're close. They get picked up and thrown in the back of a big Black Maria that drives them down to hell, where the devil sticks them on the end of his toasting fork and roasts them over the hot coals and eats them alive, and what comes out his other end gets flushed down the drain and into a lake of everlasting fire. The only way to stop this from happening is to go to confession every Saturday. That means saying sorry to God when you do bad things.'

'God save all here.'

Mrs Nagle's benediction at the doorstep was my mother's cue to shoo me upstairs so I wouldn't be putting in my spake where there was grown-ups talking. As they supped tea in the kitchen, I bellied down on the landing and earwigged on the gossip. There were biscuits down there; I could hear them.

My mother heaved a great sigh.

'What am I going to do with him, Phyllis?'

Because we had a visitor, she was using her telephone voice, pronouncing all her -ings. I crept all the way downstairs and peeped around the door.

'He won't come out of himself. I'm afeared

he'll grow up morbid.'

Mrs Nagle made sympathetic throat noises. She was a tall mannish woman with a loud hee-haw of a voice. Always went by Mrs, even though she'd never married. She lived in a draughty stone cottage about a quarter-mile down the road, right next to the freshwater well, the ownership of which was the subject of some dispute. Mrs Nagle maintained it was on her property and erected a *Keep Out — Private* sign at the mouth of the narrow lane that led to the pump. This didn't go down well with the locals, particularly Harry Farrell.

At that time, Harry was an impudent jack-of-all-trades who could be seen riding his Honda 50 around the back roads at all hours of the day or night. He took a shine to my mother and was always offering to do jobs around the house. Every birthday without fail he sent me a tenner in an envelope. As I got bigger, it became a twenty. My mother made me put most of it in the post office. Said he was like the godfather I never had.

Harry was a hard worker when he was sober. My mother sometimes got him to chop logs or strim the hedge or take clippers to the overhanging trees. But when he hit the drink he'd hock his bike and tools and chainsaw and stay in the pubs until he ran out of money, at which point he'd sleep for a week, straighten up and go looking for work all over again.

Harry — or Har The Barrel as he became known when his weight ballooned after finally giving up the drink for good — was livid when he saw Mrs Nagle's hand-painted *Keep Out* sign. He could be heard arguing in Donahue's that the well had been public property since god was a boy and that old biddy had no claim on it. And when he was really jarred he'd brag that since the day that sign went up, he never passed the well without availing of the opportunity to tap his bladder, polluting its crystal waters with his own off-yellow tributary. When Mrs Nagle got wind of this affront, she flew into a rage and, according to my mother, requisitioned a hurling stick from some young lad on the way home from school, stalked into the village and prowled from pub to pub until she found Har, whereupon she bet him from one end of the street to the other, bet him scaldy. Since that day, a savage grudge festered in Har's heart.

'What age is the chap?' Mrs Nagle brayed, adjusting her wool knit hat, the one that looked like the base of an acorn turned upside down.

'Seven,' my mother replied. 'No, eight.'

'The age of reason.' Mrs Nagle dunked a digestive and took a bite. Maybe a Marietta.

'Put him out in the fresh air,' she said, biscuit pulp bulging her cheek. 'Sunlight is nature's tonic. It cures rickets, goitre, skin conditions, ulcers and certain cancers. He'll grow feeble if he stays inside all day. Simple-minded.'

The sibilance sprayed soggy crumbs on the good tablecloth.

'He should be *vigorous*.'

'Vigorous,' my mother repeated, tearing the filter off a Major.

Mrs Nagle nodded.

'Mm-hm. The young men now are not like the young men in our time, Lily. They're pure fools in comparison.'

The rasp of a match.

'You're not wrong, Phyllis.'

My mother had her humouring voice on, like when I'd gab her ear off but she wasn't really paying attention.

'Know what I put it down to, Lily?'

'Tell me, Phyllis.'

'Porter. Drink is the proven causation of dropsy, jaundice, gout, colic, peevish irritability, catarrhs of the mouth and stomach. It's the ruination of young men. The reason they won't do a tap of work, god blast 'em for chaps.'

17

And my mother said: '*How much more abominable and filthy is man, which drinketh iniquity like water.*'

But Mrs Nagle always had to get the last word in.

'The devil has no end of work for those hands.'

So after that I got rooted out of bed early to help weed the flowerbeds and pick blackberries and all kinds of outside stuff. At that hour it was so cold the air tasted like it was doused with mint. Berry juice stung the briar cuts and nettle welts on my hands. And because the sky had been rumbling like a big belly during the night, my mother had mushrooms on the brain.

'The three things you need for mushroom picking,' she said, 'are thunder, rain and cow-dung.'

We struck off for the far bog. My mother took great yard-long strides across the wet grass and clutched a punnet to her chest. I hurried in her footsteps, hair cowslicked with morning mist. We squelched across marshy wallow ground, circumnavigating a still pond filmed with green scum and circled by midges and gadflies. My mother pointed out all the different kinds of moss and fungus, puffballs and toadstools, lichen and liverwort, reeds and rushes and bulrushes, wrack and bladderwrack. She grasped the top rung of a five-bar gate, about to mount it, but just before pulling herself up she stopped and cocked her head.

'Whisht.'

We took root, listening.

'I don't hear anything,' I whispered.

'Shhht.'

Some sort of mewling. She put her punnet down.

'A kitten maybe.'

Her eyes searched the humps of grass. Again, that sound, small and hurt and pitiful.

She peered into the gripe and pointed to a bed of briars. A hare, stretched out, its eyes swollen and suppurating, like soft wounds.

'Is it sick?' I said.

'Mixo.'

She took out her fags, cupped a match and sucked in smoke and contemplated the hare. Its hindquarters were caked with dried scutter.

'We may put it out of its misery,' she said. 'Break its neck.'

Her hand rested on my shoulder.

'You may do it, son. My nerves are not up to it.'

I stepped back, shaking my head.

'I can't.'

19

'You have to. It's not fair to let it suffer.'

My fingers were sweaty. I wiped them on my trousers.

'I thought killing was a sin.'

'Not if it's a mercy killing.'

I didn't want to go anywhere near the sick hare, but I had to obey my mother.

'All right,' I said.

She squeezed my shoulder.

'Good man. Do it quick.'

I crouched down beside the hare, peering deep into the bleeding wells of its eyes. I lunged and snatched it up by the scruff. It bucked weakly as both my hands closed around its neck.

'Not like that.' My mother rolled her eyes. 'I said *break* its neck, not choke it.'

She mimed snapping a stick of kindling.

I adjusted my grip and squeezed my eyes shut. I drove my knee into the back of the hare's neck and pulled the head and belly towards me simultaneously. There was a sound like a knuckle crack. The hare took fit. I tossed it on the grass and watched its body twitch and finally go limp. My mother got the toe of her boot under the belly, hefted her leg and sent the hare's corpse arcing into the ditch.

'C'mon,' she said. 'Those mushrooms won't pick themselves.'

The big old crow invaded my dreams. I didn't know where he'd come from or what he was supposed to mean.

He spirals out of a hole in the belly of heaven from which the angered gods cast him, to helicopter-hover, bone tired and hungry and scanning for carrion.

See how far he has fallen. Once there was wind and thunder when he flapped his wings. Huns and heathens feared him. He heralded the sun into the sea and down through the underworld, and lent his form to Morrigan, goddess of war and fate and death, who wore his cloak as she flew low over the battlefields, spurring her warriors to berserker fits and spasms.

What happened, Old Crow?

Maybe it was as St Golowin said: once upon a time you sported brightly coloured wings, but after Adam and Eve's banishment from Eden you took to eating the flesh of dead things and it turned your feathers black.

Is that it?

But the old black crow doesn't answer, merely fixes me with baleful yellow eyes,

21

beats *his wings against the walls of my dream until the walls fall down, and, stretched to the full of his span, he flaps and cackles and then he's gone.*

2

Another year on earth.

Winter melted under drizzle and gave way to the first fine day of spring. My mother pulled on her work boots, sleeves rolled up, hands sheathed in rubber gloves.

'For once and for all,' she said, flexing her fingers, 'I'm going to put manners on this garden.'

She attacked the overgrowth with a slash-hook, decapitating pismires, cut stalks oozing the white ichors of wart treatment. She squatted, skirt bunched up, rocked back on her haunches and wrenched up weeds. She planted her foot on the blade of a spade and overturned the borders, scoured the marl for earthworms and slugs, tossed their bodies onto squirming, itching piles. And when the garden was divested of weeds, and the soil smitten and chastised beneath her boots, she planted a clay-smeared hand against the small of her back and lit a fag and appraised her day's work.

Next morning she arrived back from Purcell's Nurseries with a box of shrubs and cuttings and planted them in the ground, her hands as precise as an artist's.

'Now,' she said.

'Now what?'

'We wait.'

Spring bloomed, the world exploding with wildflowers, and our garden glowed, as though incensed. My mother shaped and tended it and sat out after work as the soil exhaled vapours breathed into its pores by the daylong sun. She plucked four petals from the rose bush and placed them in cruciform across her palm.

'Look,' she said. 'The rosy cross.'

My mother among the flowers.

One stark morning, colder than usual, we looked out and saw the flowers were stricken by a late fall of frost, their frail remains preserved in sepulchral white. My mother pulled a coat on over her nightgown and walked through the deathly petals, her garden's garlands turned to shrivelled wreaths. Disappointment pained her face for a moment, but she banished it with a throw of the head.

'That's the way,' she said, and fumbled for her packet of fags. 'Things die so things are born.'

A flick of lighter flint.

'We'll plant more shrubs in the morning.'

One day soon after my tenth birthday Har Farrell called to the back door.

'Is your mother around?'

He had on an oilskin coat over baggy pants tucked inside green Wellington boots, a big brawny man with a muttonhead on him, smelling of sweat and yeast or hops.

'She's still at work,' I said.

He tipped his head in the direction of the back yard.

'C'mere a second.'

Outside, he'd placed a vicious-looking implement on the chopping block. Propped beside it, a quiver full of arrows.

'Know what this is?'

His breath reeked of the pub, a grown-up smell that suggested a world of unshaven men and darts tournaments and late-night lamping expeditions.

'It's a bow and arrow,' I said.

A smile creased his coarsely stubbled cheeks.

'Close enough. What you're looking at is a hundred and sixty-five pounds of crossbow rifle.'

He picked the weapon up and lovingly ran thick fingers over its various mechanisms.

'Here you've got your trigger,' he said. 'Here you've got your string and cable system. And heeeere — this is the cherry on top, John — an adjustable rifle sight. In theory, she should fire a couple of hundred

25

feet with reasonable accuracy, depending on who's using it of course. Those are alloy arrows. Keep the quiver waxed and you'll get indefinite use out of her. Happy birthday, son.'

He placed the crossbow in my hands. It felt like a very important moment. Like he was bequeathing me some sacred artifact in a tribal rite of passage.

'You're giving this to me?'

He nodded and beamed.

'How does it work?'

He took the crossbow, braced the stock against his shoulder, hauled the bowstring back along the bolt groove with both his hands and cocked it evenly on the latch. Then he plucked an arrow from the quiver and placed it in the breech.

'Like that,' he said, a bit unsteady on his feet. 'Pick a target.'

I scanned the yard and pointed to a tree sticking out of the back ditch.

Har thrust the crossbow back into my hands. He got behind my shoulder and helped me take aim.

'The string centre has to align with the track,' he said, 'otherwise the shot will be off. Remember, the arrow obeys the string, not the bow.'

He arranged my arms like he was Geppetto.

'For best shooting stance,' he said, 'tuck

your elbow against your hip, left hand supporting the bow here at the trigger end. You have to lean backwards a bit in order to achieve what's called the point of optimum balance. Safety off. And hold it tight.'

He patted my right pectoral.

'There's a kick off that thing'll break your shoulder if you're not careful. Ready?'

'I think so.'

'Shoot.'

I pulled the trigger. The recoil threw me off balance. The arrow left the track with an exclamatory thunk, sliced through one of my mother's slips hanging from the washing line and sailed into the next field.

'Fuck,' Har said. 'Sorry. Never mind, you'll soon get the hang of it.' He clapped me on the back. 'Just don't point it at anyone.'

As soon as he left, I wrapped the crossbow and quiver in a coal sack and hid it in the cubbyhole under the stairs.

There was a caterpillar and a wasp inside the jamjar. The wasp was ramming his stingers, what Harper called *ovipositors*, into the caterpillar, injecting eggs through the gaps in its exoskeleton. The caterpillar went into shock. When the wasp finished its business I screwed the lid off and let it fly off. It body-swerved into my mother, returning from the clinic. She swatted at the wasp and continued moving unsteadily up the front path, picking her steps like she was fording a stony stream. Her face was a fright. I'd never seen her look so shook. I asked her what was for dinner, not because I wanted to know, but because I wanted her to return to her normal self. She shook her head and stepped around me and went into the kitchen, moving like she was in a trance. The kettle went on, then the wireless. I shook the jar to try and get a rise out of the caterpillar. No response.

My mother set the fire and made the dinner and called me inside when it was on the table. I ran upstairs and stashed the jar in my bedroom and went to wash my hands.

My mother sipped from her teacup and looked out the window while I ate. She left her own plate mostly untouched. The fire crackled and the sacred heart glowed on the mantelpiece.

'Son,' she said, 'we need to talk.'

I shovelled food in. Hot. I fanned a hand in front of my mouth.

'Uh-huh?'

'I have to go away for a little while soon.'

'Where to?'

'The hospital.'

My fork went down. It was getting dark outside and the wind moaned in the chimney.

Winter was coming.

'Why?'

'I have to go for a little rest. It won't be long. Only a week or so.'

'A *week?*'

An awful empty feeling spread through my stomach. Beside the potted geraniums, Haircut Charlie idiot-grinned atop the windowsill, bizarre tufts of green hair shooting upwards from his perforated skull.

'Why don't you just go upstairs for a lie down?' I said. 'Why do you have to go to the hospital?'

She shook her head, set down her cup.

'Listen. I've arranged for Mrs Nagle to come and mind you. While I'm gone, I need you to be good. It won't be long. When I come home everything will be the way it was. *An dtigeann tú?*'

'*Tigim.*'

My mother took a taxi to the hospital. I went to school as per normal and Mrs Nagle came in the afternoons to make dinner. The food was the same, but it tasted different, slightly burnt. Plus, she left the door open when she used the toilet, and I could see her old lady tights puddled around her veiny ankles and thick brown brogues. The same brogues I heard creaking outside when it was my turn to use the bathroom.

Mrs Nagle sent me to bed early most nights so she could watch the telly and shovel chocolates in her mouth. I lay awake and stared at the ceiling and thought about what they could be doing to my mother in the hospital. Every so often I checked the jamjar glass and watched for signs of what was happening inside the caterpillar's body cavity. I waited for the wasp eggs to hatch, imagining the larvae as they tapped into the caterpillar's energy sources, draining it of the will to live, or reproduce, making its little testicles shrivel so it wouldn't want to have any more caterpillar sex. Drinking its blood and devouring everything but the vital organs. If I waited long enough, I'd get to see the larvae burrow out and turn into baby wasps. I'd see the caterpillar's body crumble like the ash on a gone-out fag. And I'd throw open the window and let the baby wasps escape, the caterpillar's death unrevenged by Mother Nature, because Mother Nature doesn't care.

When my mother came home she moved like an old woman and had to take salt baths every evening. One time she called me into the bathroom, I was mortified, but her female parts were all covered with towels, except for where the scar rose up from her lower belly, white-lipped like a Nazi's smile.

'That's from the operation,' she said.

I grunted something in response and made my excuses and left her to her bath.

Even though my mother was on the mend, Mrs Nagle insisted on staying on a bit longer.

'Just till you get back on your feet,' she said. 'I insist.'

That whole time, the house hissed with women's whispering. I hid out in my room and read comics and drew pictures of crows or worms. After a couple of weeks my mother got well enough to go back to work, but Mrs Nagle showed no sign of leaving. No matter how many hints my mother dropped, it didn't seem to register, until one morning there was a row and Mrs Nagle stormed out, complaining that people don't appreciate a good turn any more, and bad luck to the lot of us.

After she left, things got back to normal.

But nothing felt the same.

One night I dreamed there was a nuclear war that blackened and charred the earth. Everything went medieval and the few humans left alive were terrorised and preyed on by giant mutant crows the size of pterodactyls. They plagued the skies like flocks of swastikas, pestering the heavens with their questions.

Cá? Cá?

My native name was Crow Killer John and it was my job to keep the giant birds from preying on the people of my tribe. All day long I stalked the fields around our settlement, keeping watch from the tops of cairns and crannógs, Har's crossbow in hand, protecting the little ones from circling scaldcrows and daws and magpies as big as aircraft cawing *where-where-where* over and over, their beady eyes trained on us juicy humans, peepers peeled for easy pickings.

Hunger got the better of one fat jackal-eyed boyo. He spotted me and swooped in low. I braced the crossbow stock against my shoulder, closed one eye and focused.

Remember: the arrow obeys the string, not the bow.

The crow loomed huge in the crosshairs.

Closer still, beak open wide, crazy-brained with hunger.

I counted off the seconds.

One.

Two.

Two and a half.

My trigger finger whitened.

Pull!

The arrow took flight, a lightning bolt, skewering the crow. He plummeted to the earth and twitched and flapped and spurted weird green blood as if he were a lawn sprinkler.

'Ha!' I said.

The rest of the pack scattered in panic, but it took them only a moment to regroup. The sky blackened. Some of the crows fell on their fallen comrade and ripped his carcass apart, entrails dripping from their beaks. Others jeered and mocked and prepared to attack.

I dipped into the quiver, extracted another arrow, pulled back the bowstring. Through the crossbow's scope I saw a big black bastard of a hobo crow, bigger than the rest. My finger froze on the trigger. His eyes were huge, like twin kaleidoscopes, whirling and turning and glowing like yellow coals. He opened his beak, and when he spoke it was as if his voice was alive inside my mind.

Sometimes the worm turns, John. Sometimes it turns into a serpent.

Hypnotised, I couldn't tear my eyes away. My hands wouldn't obey me. They turned the crossbow around until its cold muzzle was in my mouth, my thumb curled around the trigger.

Pull.

Slumped at the table, humidified by porridge steam, I saw my face in the glass milk jug, sullen, squinty eyes underscored by blue shadows. Skin erupting with angry black-and-whiteheads. The first growth of stubble struggling on the upper lip and chin. My voice had broken and returned an octave deeper. I was thirteen. The world didn't like me.

'John.' My mother's voice was megaphoned by her mug. 'Are you familiar with Leviticus 15?'

I shovelled porridge into my mouth.

'Not off the top of my head.'

'It says, *When any man hath a running issue out of his flesh, because of his issue he is unclean.*' She put her cup down and cleared her throat. 'Tell me son, have you been given to certain acts of, ah, self-pollution.'

A lump of oatmeal went down wrong. I coughed and wheezed and spluttered. She reached over and thumped my shoulders.

'Only you've lately developed symptoms of the chronic self-abuser.'

I brought up the lump. She stopped with the thumping. The forefinger of her right hand depressed each digit of the left in turn.

'You've taken to shunning company.'

That was the pinkie.

'I hear you wandering around the house at all hours.'

Ring finger.

'You have saddlebags under your eyes, and you won't so much as look at me.'

Middle.

'Your hands do be shaking.'

Index.

'And you've gone away to nothing.'

Thumb.

I hawked and cleared my throat. My lungs still felt clogged with watery oatmeal.

'Ma,' I said, 'you sound like Mrs Nagle.'

I went back to spooning porridge, but she rapped the table to get my attention.

'*If any man's seed of copulation go out from him, then he shall wash all his flesh in water, and be unclean until the even. And every garment, and every skin, whereon is the seed of copulation, shall be washed with water, and be unclean until the even.* Deuteronomy. Or Leviticus. I forget which.'

She stared into the infinity over my left shoulder.

'A good honeycomb sponge bath would sort you out.'

She sipped her tea and peered slyly over the rim of the mug.

'Sure I remember you used to spray like a hose when I changed your nappy.'

There was an almost wistful smile playing about her lips. A porridge blob plopped from my mouth into the bowl. I couldn't tell whether or not this whole routine was some kind of joke. I wasn't sure she knew herself. She sighed, fingers twisting her hair, and said, 'John, are you having fantasies? About girls?'

'No.'

'Boys?'

'Maaaa!'

That came out as a bleat. She raised an eyebrow and smirked.

'A *sheep?*'

Whenever my mother suspected something astray, her cure tended to be more painful than the ailment. Like the time she prised a splinter from my hand with a sewing needle sterilised over her lighter. Or when I got a blister on my heel from wearing new shoes and she burst it with her fingernails and sprinkled the tender new skin with salt.

'Did I ever tell you the story of Labhra Loingseach,' she said, 'the king with donkey's ears? According to the legend, any barber who cut the King Labhra's hair was put to death afterwards so they couldn't reveal his secret. But this one barber begged to be spared for the sake of his wife and children. The king took pity on him and agreed to let him live so long as he didn't breathe a word.

36

The barber agreed, but as the days went by, he was driven mad by the thought of what was under Labhra Loingseach's hair, so he went out into the woods and threw his arms around a tree and whispered his secret into a knot in the wood. But one of the court musicians asked a tree-cutter to chop the tree down for wood to make a harp, and when he played the harp in the court of the king, a voice rang out: *Labhra Loingseach's got donkey's ears.* Then all the trees of the forest joined in and the king fled his castle in mortification.'

She patted the back of my hand.

'Y'know, secrets have a way of coming out in their own time. So tell me. What's keeping you up at nights?'

I couldn't put up with any more. I told her.

'I have bad dreams sometimes, that's all.'

She blinked. That's all she did. Her face zoomed in so close I could smell the smoke on her breath.

'About what?'

I shook my head and lifted spoonfuls of cold slop and let them gloop into the bowl.

'Nothing. Just stupid stuff.'

My mother's eyes blazed across the room. They took in the fire, the coal bucket, the sacred-heart lamp, Haircut Charlie. They peered through the window at the trees outside. And they lit on the television set on the counter.

'That fecken thing,' she said, her face stony with resolve. 'The devil's teat.'

I had no idea what she was on about.

She crossed the kitchen, yanked the plug from the socket, grappled the television off the counter and wobbled across the floor.

'Open the door,' she grunted.

'What are you doing?'

'What I should've done long ago. Now open the door and do as you're bid.'

I got up and pulled the door open wide. She staggered outside and set the television down on the front path, the flex coiled on the ground like a three-pronged tail.

'I'm selling that thing. And no more about it.'

She made good on her threat. Later that afternoon, Har Farrell came to collect it. Money changed hands. But it didn't cure me of the dreams.

The church steeple looms over the village of Kilcody, God's lightning rod. The old crow's claws are clamped to the weathervane at its summit. He prances about, a child doing the wee-wee dance, ruffles the black boa of his feathers and glowers at the people below as they shuffle through the chapel arch.

A gust rotates the weathervane slowly through four points of the compass. West across The Holla, the mountains stand shoulder to shoulder like ogre brothers. Up north, the Waxon factory discharges gaggles of haggard, fag-lipped girls and denim-jacketed hard chaws. Southerly, The Ginnet, the library, Tyrell's bike shop. And then beyond the river and the railway tracks, the east road runs seaward through five miles of fields, headlong into the waves.

The crow's sonar sweeps the nearabouts. A flap of black and he glides over the headstones jutting from the gummy loam, over the head of the great stone angel set on a plinth at the centre of the cemetery, and he leaves the humans to their human doings.

3

Most boys are all balls and elbows and bad moods when they turn fifteen, and I was no exception. My mother sometimes expressed misgivings that I had no friends my own age, but I was content with my own company, kept my head perpetually buried in comics and paperbacks poached from the stall outside the secondhand shop on Barracks Street.

Sometimes I spent the after school hours at the library reading encyclopedias and old religious books remaindered from St Patrick's Seminary in Ballo. It was hushed as a church in that sterile library light, and time passed easily among the dusty yellowed pages and faded ink. I read until my eyes felt dried and cracked and I wished there was a chip you could get implanted in your brain that would store the gist of every book ever written and you could call up the text at will, scrolling the pages down your mind's eye.

But when the weather grew hot and sticky and everywhere the sap was rising it was harder to concentrate, so I killed time hanging around the mini-arcade in Fernie's shop where spotty, goggle-eyed lads pumped coppers into the old Space Invaders. Or else I mooched around the market square where country chaps waited for their bus, ties off and sleeves rolled up. Those were the last days of term, the doss days just before the summer exams when the heat was intimate and the air sweet with mowed grass.

That's when I met Jamey.

'*Hoy.*'

I heard the voice before I caught sight of the face, whirled in a 180-degree pan trying to pinpoint the source. He was parked like a big barnacle at the base of the Father Carthy monument. There was a book balanced on his lap, and an unlit fag jutted from his mouth.

'You with the head,' he said, placing his book on the ledge. 'Got a light?'

I wasn't in the habit of buying cigarettes, not yet, but I carried matches for chewing on, or skewering woodlice. He detached himself from Father Carthy's shadow and stood to take them from me. His shape's molecules, his very stuff, seemed to shift and recombine in the sunlight.

'I'm Jamey Corboy,' he said.

He offered me a smoke. I wavered a bit, but he insisted.

'I've loads. I broke into The Ginnet a couple of weeks ago. Came out with four bottles of vodka and six cartons of fags.'

That was a lot to tell someone you've just met, but I put no pass on it. I took the cigarette and he lit us both. The taste of smoke was sour in my mouth and its effects made me feel a bit nauseous.

Jamey had on a Crombie coat that came to his shins. Black jeans and army boots, floppy hair raked back from a high forehead and a somewhat beaky nose. His eyes were intensely blue, almost frightened, and if you touched him, he'd jump.

'I hope we don't get the weather you're expecting,' I said. 'You must be roasted.'

He flicked ash on the ground.

'I don't dress for the weather.'

He was a blow-in from Ballo town, a year ahead of me, just about to start his Junior Cert. Like all transplants he was something of a loner, the only boy who sat in the school shelter writing in a spiral notebook instead of stampeding around the yard after a bursted football. He lived in one of the nice houses on Summer Hill, the ones with the trimmed lawns and palm trees.

The teachers said he had brains to burn but couldn't be motivated. When I got to know him a bit better he told me he was adopted and that when his younger brother came along it was like he didn't exist any more. People always thought he was older than he was. That got him served in pubs; the confident way he carried himself.

Across the road in front of Brown's Hardware, barelegged heifers from the Mercy were playing arses and kicks. Mister Brown came out and ran them. Jamey watched all this, a smile tempting the corner of his mouth.

I nodded at his book.

'What you reading?'

He picked it up and flipped the pages.

'*Rimbaud in Africa.*'

'Who's Rimbaud?'

'A writer.'

He clawed hair out of his eyes.

'Brainy bugger. Revolutionised poetry by the time he was twenty-one, then jacked it all in and bunked off to Africa and made a fortune running guns and slave-trading.'

He waved his hands around as he spoke, the smoke describing swirls and spirals in the air.

'Him and his buddies used to drink absinthe in a kip called The Dead Rat in Paris. One time Rimbaud climbed up on the table, dropped his pants and took a dump and painted a picture in it. Big into blasphemy too, used to carve graffiti into park benches. *Merde à Dieu.*'

'What's that mean?'

'Look it up.'

'I will.'

I stooped and plucked *Harper's Compendium* from my schoolbag.

'Here's what I'm reading.'

Jamey took a pair of glasses from his shirt pocket and perched them on his nose. They were round and wire-rimmed and completely transformed his face, made him look more owlish. He thumbed through the pages.

'Man,' he said, eyes glowing behind the lenses, 'this is some strange.'

He flipped to the plates and gawped at an illustration of a tapeworm exiting a snail.

'Oh Jesus, that's fucking repulsive.'

Then he pointed to a picture of a maggot curled up in some brain.

'What *is* this? Worm porn? You *like* this stuff?'

I shrugged.

'Nature's pretty twisted.'

He shut the book and thrust it back in my hands.

'I'm sorry, man, I can't look at that.'

He shuddered like he had to pee, dropped his cigarette and squashed it beneath his boot.

Outside Brown's Electrical a gypsy-looking bloke in a porkpie hat began to play the accordion, the instrument case open at his feet. A few youngsters clustered around and began to flick coins at him. Somebody grabbed the case and started to drag it down the path. The musician shouted and made a grab for it. Someone else picked it up and ran, and the musician chased after him awkwardly, the accordion still strapped around his chest.

Jamey rubbed his chin. There was a ring on the fourth finger of his right hand. Some kind of stone, maybe garnet.

'Hey,' he said, 'want to hear something? It's right up your alley.'

I was starting to feel conspicuous talking to this weird kid in the middle of the market square, but it wasn't like I had anything else to do.

'Go on then.'

'This girl, Annie.' He plucked a flake of tobacco from between his tongue and teeth and flicked it away. 'One morning she woke up with an itch that she couldn't quite scratch, right down in the basement of the ladies' department. An irritation. It got so bad she had to make an appointment to see her doctor. Next thing she was sitting in the waiting room looking at the eye chart and the two letters V and D started *glowing* at her.'

'Why?'

'Venereal Disease. The clap. But she was thinking that couldn't be the trouble, cos she and the boyfriend were using protection. Besides, he was a virgin when they met. His name was Gavin and his big ambition was someday he'd become the state pathologist. She had a thing for nerds. A lot of girls do, you'd be surprised.'

'I know.'

I didn't know.

'Anyhow, they were at it like rabbits at first, but the sex life cooled off a bit when he took a second job. Stress, man. It's a killer. So she was thinking it must be something harmless, like a yeast infection.'

His eyes shone as he spoke, that half-smile on his lips. Watching the way his whole body seemed to engage with the telling of the story provided as much amusement as the story itself.

'So she arrived into the waiting room, dreading the examination. She'd known the doctor since he gave her the BCG. Pure melt. But she told him the problem, and the doctor had a good poke around, and when he was finished he said, 'Annie, do you have a regular sexual partner?'

Jamey was getting so into the story now, bubbles of spit had begun to form around the corners of his mouth.

'When she said yes, he asked where this boyfriend could be found. She told him: 'Park Road Funeral Home.' The doc nodded his head, as if that explained everything. And Annie said, 'Doctor, what's that louser given me?' And the doc just said, 'You don't need to know that right now.' But she insisted. 'Whatever it is, I need to know,' she said. 'I mean, is it terminal?' And the doc closed his eyes a second and said, 'No, Annie. Not for you anyway.' '

'And?' I said.

'Ah?'

'What did she have?'

'Maggots.'

My mother was scrubbing potatoes at the kitchen sink, placing the clean ones in a colander on the draining board. She scoured the skins and gouged out the eyes with a knife, then began to slice onions on a chopping board. When she sensed my presence, she turned, and her eyes were red and filled with water from the stinging onion juice. She wiped her face with the rolled-up sleeve of her cardigan.

'What's for dinner?' I said.

'Pig's feet and hairy buttermilk.'

She sounded tired. She filled the big saucepan to the halfway mark from the tap, hefted it onto the cooker with a grunt and wiped her hands on the tea towel.

'Saw you in town today,' she said.

Town. She always called Kilcody a town.

'You were knocking around with that young Corboy.'

She turned, and her face looked drawn and puffy-eyed.

'You were smoking.'

I didn't reply, just stood radiating guilt. She pulled a chair out, sat at the table and plucked a Silk Cut Light from its packet. Her latest brand. Pregnant women's fags, she called them. She tore off the filter and screwed it into the holder.

'These fecken things.'

Here comes the sermon, I thought. The gospel according to Mrs Nagle, regarding the injurious effects of tobacco smoking. How it causes diseases of the vital organs, heartburn, nausea, belching, diarrhoea, shortness of breath, heart palpitations, oppression of the chest and back pain. How it can incur drowsiness, paralysis, unnatural sleep and bad dreams.

But she didn't say anything, just smoked the cigarette down to the writing while I waited, not knowing whether to go on up to my room or stay put.

At last she squished the fag butt into the

49

seashell on the table. She took a match and poked it into the holder, moving it clockwise. When she took the match out, the tip was smeared with what looked like black earwax.

'See that?' she said. 'That's tar. Smoke enough fags, that's what your lungs fill up with.'

She placed the soiled match in the ashtray.

'They'll kill you, son. Give 'em up while you can. Do you hear me talking to you?'

'Yeah.'

'Good. Go on.'

I mounted the stairs.

'And son.'

'What?'

She was staring off into middle distance, face unreadable, smoke around her head like some dissipating halo.

'Stay away from that Jamey Corboy.'

The last week of school, Jamey invited me around to his house to have a look at his books and maybe borrow a couple. There was no answer when I knocked the front door, so I pushed open the letterbox and peered inside.

'Hullo?'

A woman appeared in the hall, wide-screened by the rectangular flap. She was pretty in a brittle sort of way, bottle-blond hair secured by a banana clip in a high ponytail that pulled the skin so tight it could've been a facelift.

'Hello there,' she said as she opened the door, willowy and clean in a pale blue summer dress. She looked me up and down with cat-green eyes. I cleared my throat and tried to look as harmless as possible. Parents are easily fooled. All you need are manners.

'I'm John,' I said. 'A friend of Jamey's.'

My voice had gone up a semitone of its own accord.

'Ah, yes.' Her eyes twinkled a bit. 'Come in. I'm Deirdre. Dee for short.'

Deirdre — Dee — spoke over her shoulder as I wiped my feet on the doormat.

'I'm glad Jamey's made a friend here,' she said. 'I was worried he'd never settle in.'

She called up the stairs and turned and put her hand on my arm.

'I'm sorry, but I've forgotten your name already. You must think I'm awful rude.'

'John.'

'Of course.'

A door opened upstairs, you could hear what sounded like cartoon music for the insane, screeching and caterwauling, and Jamey came down the steps two at a time.

'Hey worm-boy,' he said loudly.

Dee's brow wrinkled at the nickname. She

released her grip on my arm and rubbed her forehead lightly as if to smooth the creases. She was about to say something, thought the better of it, gave her head a little twitch, like whatever had occurred to her was a midge that needed shaking off.

''Scuse me,' she said, moving towards the kitchen. 'I've dinner on.'

Jamey was in his stocking feet. He looked at my runners.

'Did she not ask you to take your shoes off?'

'No.'

He exhaled through his nose.

Their kitchen was bright and airy. The counter gleamed and all the appliances looked shiny and new. It didn't smell like my house. It smelled of no smell at all, anodyne.

Jamey spooned instant coffee into a couple of mugs, poured the milk and stirred it all into a paste before adding boiling water from the kettle. His mother bustled about collecting keys and things.

'I have to pick up your brother,' she said. 'I'll be back in a few minutes.'

She gave Jamey a look as she hurried out.

'Try to keep the noise down.'

There was a constant push and pull going on between Jamey and his mother, an undertow. I noticed it even that first day. The things they said to each other were like the tips of jagged ice floes, only a fraction of the true mass apparent.

Jamey handed me a cup with a picture of Lady Di on it.

'Come on up,' he said, jerking his head.

Thick carpet muffled our footsteps on the stairs and landing. Their whole house looked like it had been serviced by one of those domestic robots you'd see in some futuristic film where a master computer wakes you up with chilled-out classical music, makes your morning coffee and puts water on for the shower. The walls had a fresh paint job and the laundry was stacked neatly in a hamper, no stray socks or shoes strewn about. I felt like a walking rubbish heap just being there.

Jamey pushed open his bedroom door with his foot, and I felt somehow reassured by the state of his room. It was even messier than my own. Piles of books and tapes were stacked in columns beside a stereo. The blinds were drawn and there was a glittery purple scarf draped on a lamp.

'I like to keep it dark in here,' Jamey said. 'The summer doesn't agree with my constitution.'

He set his cup on the windowsill beside his bed and waved a hand at a stack of old vinyl albums.

'You're the DJ.'

I didn't recognize any of the names.

'You pick something,' I said. 'I'm not much on music.'

That wasn't exactly true. I listened to the radio all the time, but I was still a bit intimidated by Jamey. He had more albums than I'd ever seen.

He ran his thumb over the sleeves, selected a record and changed the music. Electronic sounds seemed to liquefy and run from the stereo's speakers, a slippery, mercurial language I couldn't grasp. He sat cross-legged on the floor and began to pass me books. *A Season in Hell* by Rimbaud. Dante's *Inferno*. A broken-spined *Les Fleurs du mal* with hungry-looking orchids on the cover. I placed the books to one side.

'Your mother wasn't what I expected,' I said. 'I thought she'd be a bit more . . . '

'What?'

'Suspicious.'

Jamey laughed.

'Dee likes to think the best about people. She's funny that way.'

Jamey always referred to his parents by their first names. There was no way I could imagine calling my mother Lily.

'A bit high-strung though. Spends more money on anti-bacterial wipes than she does on food. Maurice is just as bad. Typical dentist. Did you know that dentists have one of the highest suicide rates of any profession? I reckon it's from looking in people's filthy mouths all day long. All that bad breath and cruddy teeth would drive anyone to the brink.'

He waved a hand vaguely at the adjoining room.

'You want to see his study. The walls are covered with these pictures of oral diseases, abscesses and ulcers and stuff. He used to be a boxer, can you believe that? Apparently he was pretty nifty with his fists when he was a kid. Some of the trainers even thought he could try out for the Olympic team, only he quit when he was about my age. Went from knocking people's teeth out to putting them back in.'

He fell silent, and the music rose to fill the space.

'Y'know, I think Dee might be cheating on him.'

The skin at the back of my neck prickled.

'Really?'

He pursed his lips and slowly nodded.

'Either she has, or she's about to.'

Jamey put his back to the edge of the bed and pulled his knees up to his chin. For a moment all the self-assurance vanished.

'A couple of months ago I was upstairs in Donahue's,' he said quietly. 'It's like this disco bar, they've an extension at the weekends. One night during the Easter holidays I went in there to see if there was anything stirring, you know, chick-wise.'

His voice wobbled and he had to clear his throat before going on.

'Dee was, um . . . '

'What?'

'Dancing. In the middle of a crowd of blokes. And she was wearing this little black dress. Like a cocktail dress.'

I pictured Dee in a little black number. She was in pretty good shape.

'Did anything happen?'

He sort of grimaced.

'I didn't hang around.'

We sat and listened to the music and drank our coffee. After a few minutes we felt the front door slam and heard stomping up the stairs.

'Here comes his lordship,' Jamey said. 'We'll get no peace now.'

The door burst open and his little brother barrelled in, a chubby moon-faced youngster with a thick mop of hair, huge eyes and an even bigger grin. He threw his arms around Jamey, who hugged him back.

'Ollie,' he said, 'I want you to meet a friend

of mine. This is John.'

The boy stared at me, his belly bulging beneath a bright blue T-shirt with a yellow Superman insignia. His chin was shiny with dribble. He grabbed my sleeve and started to tug.

'Cartoons,' he said.

'What's that?'

He tugged harder.

'Cartooons.'

Jamey translated.

'He wants us to watch television with him.'

He gently began to push his little brother out of the room.

'Not now, Ollie. Me and John need to talk.'

'Cartooons,' the boy shouted.

'I'll watch them with you later,' Jamey said firmly. 'I promise.'

He shooed Ollie out onto the landing and shut the door.

'Jesus,' I said. 'What a live wire.'

There was a knock on the door. Jamey opened it, and his brother stood there with sorrowful spaniel eyes.

Jamey shook his head and grinned.

'You just don't know when to quit, do you?'

We went into Ollie's room and sprawled among the heaped Beanie Babies and stuffed huskies and watched the cartoons on the portable television set, the boy hooting and clapping his hands. Jamey pulled a bag of apple-drops from his pocket.

'Give Ollie one of these,' he said. 'He'll be your friend for life.'

I plucked out a sticky sweet and offered it to Ollie, who took it in his grubby fingers and mechanically popped it in his mouth, eyes glued to the screen. He laughed so hard at the sight of a school of dancing jellyfish that he started to wheeze and cough, then his eyes bulged and he clawed at his throat. I looked at Jamey, who was deeply absorbed in the cartoon.

'Jamey,' I said, 'is he having a fit or something?'

He glanced at Ollie.

'Shit!'

He grabbed his brother by the shoulders and began to shake him.

'He's choking!'

Ollie was making horrible gacking noises. Before I could think, I'd knocked Jamey aside and driven the heel of my hand under the boy's breastbone, hard. Ollie pushed me off and tried to scramble away. I hit him again, harder this time, and an apple drop rocketed out of his mouth and smacked me in the forehead, and then he and Jamey were rolling around the floor laughing.

'Gotcha!' Ollie shouted, whooping and slapping his leg. 'Gotcha!'

Warm relief flooded from the centre of my stomach and tingled outwards to my hands and feet. I should've been mad at them both, but I was just grateful that the drama was over.

'Sorry, man,' Jamey said, his whole body quaking with laughter. 'It's Ollie's party piece.'

Siberia was our school nickname for Room 15, which wasn't really a room but a shabby prefab in a state of disrepair bordering on collapse, so called because it was located so far from the main school building, and in the winter it was freezing. Only one of the radiators worked and there were holes punched clear through the walls in parts, leaking chalky innards.

But now it was a Friday afternoon in early summer and everyone was restless, couldn't concentrate with the novelty heat and the promise of holidays just beyond our grasp like an idea that won't materialise. The classroom floor was strewn with an obstacle course of kitbags and big sprawgy feet, the air salt-and-vinegared with sweat. Last class English, Miss Ross the replacement teacher for Mrs Lynch, who was pregnant again.

Miss Ross, first name Molly, very early twenties, was the closest thing to good-looking among the teachers, albeit with the faintest suggestion of whippet about the nose and mouth. An almost reverent silence descended when she turned to write on the blackboard in her immaculate script, a fairly nasty poem about some nymphette getting sexually assaulted by a dirty great swan. Her bum was truly mesmerising, packed into pants so tight you could almost make out the cleavage. Wedged into the desk in front of me, lanky Gabby Mahon tugged at the front of his pants and groaned like he'd eaten too many crab-apples.

Miss Ross finished the poem with a flourish, placed her stick of chalk on the ledge and turned to face the class. The disappearance of her bottom was somewhat compensated for by her blouse being undone to the third.

'Now, boys,' she said, clapping chalkdust from her palms, 'I want you to take that down in your copies and learn the first two stanzas for Monday.'

Gabby Mahon emitted another pained sound. Miss Ross consulted the roll, still too new to have gotten the hang of our names.

'Gabriel Mahon,' she said, 'would you

stand up and read the first eight lines aloud please?'

Gabby stood, in a hoop with the blueballs, squinted at the blackboard and tried to speak. His face went pale and his eyes rolled up until you could see only whites and he took faint and had to be helped out into the bright sunlight of the yard.

And we all envied him something rotten.

The Junior Cert should have kept Jamey out of action for at least a couple of weeks, but he was one of those people who get away without doing a thing, who just cram at the last minute and sail through the papers with an ease that makes the rest of us spit nails.

A couple of days after the exams had started I was passing the café with the sign on the door advertising cut-rate long-distance calls. I saw him sitting at a table by the window. He was hunched over a Moleskine notebook, the *Ballo Valley Sentinel* and a mug of coffee set to one side, schoolbag at his feet. His granny glasses were perched on the end of his beaky nose and he was writing furiously, filling the page with reams of tiny spidery writing. Plus, he was wearing — get this — a suit. No secondhand double-breasted job with shabby cuffs and flared trousers either, but a proper three-piece, tailored to fit. He looked good. Jamey had a relationship with clothes I could never hope to emulate, seemed to apply the same set of aesthetics to them as he did to books or music. Me, I just wore whatever my mother picked up in the sales.

He spotted me watching and beckoned me inside. The coffee machine behind the counter hissed.

'How's the worm-boy,' he said, almost shouting over the din.

To be honest, the worm-boy stuff was getting a bit old. He must've sensed my irritation because that was the last time I heard it.

'You want something to drink?'

I shook my head and took a seat. He spread the *Sentinel* on the table, tapped the bottom of the front page.

'Have a look at this,' he said as he rose from his chair.

I read the article while he ordered a refill.

Local Asylum Seeker Disappears After Attack

by Jason Davin, Staff Reporter

Concerns were expressed at the sudden disappearance last week of Jude Udechukwu, a 20-year-old non-national whose last known address was at 14 Rafferty Street. Mr Udechukwu, *The Sentinel* understands, was retained in an 'off the books' capacity at a local garage. It is believed that the night before his disappearance, he was involved in an altercation with a number of locals and failed to report for work the next morning. The following day, a work colleague contacted Mr Udechukwu's landlord, Mr Thos Rackard. On gaining entry to his flat, they found that many of his personal effects were missing. 'It was odd,' Mr Rackard told *The Sentinel*. 'If he was planning on doing a runner, you'd think he would've wanted his deposit back. It's not like I was planning to keep it.'

At the time of going to press, local Gardai said they were awaiting further developments before considering mounting a search for the missing man.

'Funny how they call 'em non-nationals,' Jamey said, placing the fresh cup beside the old one. 'Like they were all born out of thin air. You ask me, he probably got fed up and buggered off back to Africa.'

Seconds later he said, 'Have you seen the new shop beside Fernie's?'

I hadn't.

'Aw, man. You should check it out. It's full of mad African stuff. Weird food and ornaments.'

He looked out the window of the café and said, almost to himself: 'This is one weirdo little village. I tell you, when I get out of this place, I'm gonna write a book about it that'll turn your hair white.'

'*I am only escaped to tell thee,*' I said.

Jamey's eyebrows arched.

'What's that?'

It was something my mother was in the habit of saying, in the important tone of voice she reserved for quotations. I repeated it and Jamey nodded.

'Why did you move up here anyway?' I said.

'Ollie. The special school is much better than the one in Ballo. Smaller classes.'

'Why is he in a special school? He seems fine to me.'

'I know. The kid's sharper than I am. It's one of Dee's . . . things. She seems to think he needs special attention. Whatever. I didn't mind moving. Ballo was boring, man. Nothing but housing estates.'

He caught sight of something over my shoulder. His face froze and he spoke in a low voice, barely moving his lips.

'Don't look, John, but some old bird is staring holes in you through the window.'

Slowly I eased around in my seat. There was a woman there, sure enough. A tall woman in a wool-knit cap. Mrs Nagle. She averted her eyes and moved off, pushing one of those shopping bags on wheels. Jamey watched her go.

'Who was that nosebag?'

'Oh, just the old woman who lived in the woods,' I said. 'A weela weela waile.'

Jamey gathered his papers and put them into his schoolbag. As he got up, he slid a large manila envelope across the table. I picked it up and peered inside.

'What's this?'

'One of my stories. Don't read it now. Wait till I'm out the door.'

He shouldered his bag and left, sharp as a blade in his three-piece suit.

The envelope contained a number of A4 sheets, handwritten and photocopied. I counted out my change and ordered a cup of tea and read through the story.

The Grace of God

by Jamey Corboy

The two o'clock extraction cancelled, so Maurice went back to his book about the Ali — Foreman fight in Zaire. When was that?

1972? '74? He could remember watching it through fuzzy reception on the black-and-white television set in the kitchen of their old bungalow. It was a tradition, staying up with his dad until the early hours to watch the big fights, the Rumble in the Jungle, the Thriller in Manilla, the Olympics, the sad travesty of Ali versus Spinks.

Maurice lived for boxing. He was barely out of short trousers when he joined the local club, St Anthony's. They said he was a natural. The old man was proud of him. Not only could he take punishment as well as dish it out, but he loved to train too, the roadwork, the thud of the bag, the smack of the pads, the *slappeta-dappeta* of the overhead ball, the smell of sweat and leather gloves.

But what he saw one afternoon in Ballo changed everything, left him so shook he never climbed inside a boxing ring again. When his father quizzed him about it, he just clammed up. Said he was done fighting and no more about it.

His mother made no secret of her relief. She'd been a bag of nerves ever since a local boy collapsed and died after a bout in Balinbagin. Fifteen years old. What was the chap's name? He couldn't remember. The post-mortem revealed some sort of blood clot on the brain that probably would've done him in sooner or later, but you couldn't tell that to all the concerned parents and protestors who wrote to the papers and lobbied the council about it. As a result, all the amateur clubs in the county came under pressure to make protective gear compulsory.

Like most of the boys, Maurice hated those big bulky head-guards. He'd worn them during sparring matches and it felt like trying to fight while wearing a crash helmet. The club's mentors could only shrug and say they didn't like it either, but what could they do? The tourney that day in Ballo was one of the last where the boys were allowed to go bare-headed.

The venue was a draughty old school hall. By the time the St Anthony's contingent arrived Maurice still wasn't assured of a match, so he tried to relax and watch the junior bouts, red-faced little urchins with snotty noses throwing wild barnyard swings. As the afternoon wore on the boxers got bigger and the quality of the fights improved. Maurice was about to start packing up his gear when Andy, one of the club's trainers, brought word.

'We've found a lad for you,' he said. 'You'd better get togged off.'

The dressing room was cluttered with stacking chairs and kitbags and towels. The air was thick with the smell of sweat and Deep Heat. Maurice got out of his tracksuit and into his singlet and shorts. He could feel his stomach tighten, a tingling around the back of his neck. He thought of Our Lord in the garden of Gethsemane, sweating blood, and then of the old saying about how you should never bet money on a boxer who crosses himself before a fight, because any fighter relying on the grace of god is a dead duck.

'Let's get you bandaged up,' said Andy, a spry man in his thirties, wiry and small as a jockey, a handy bantamweight in his time. He took two new rolls of bandages from his tracksuit bottoms, tore a hole in the end of one of the rolls, slipped it over Maurice's thumb and began wrapping the knuckles with practised expertise, swaddling between the fingers, encircling the wrist, tying off the ends.

'Make a fist.'

Maurice flexed.

'Too tight?'

'Nope.'

Andy started on the other hand, talking as he worked.

'This chap's name is Timmy Breen,' he said. 'He has a few inches on you, so you'll need to be nifty. Don't go toe to toe. Jab and move. If you land, don't stand there like a daw admiring your handiwork. Jab, jab, jab, then a right hook to the ribs. Boom-boom!'

He bounced back on his heels and mimed a flurry of lethal-looking punches.

'Where's your gumshield?'

Maurice took it out of his kit bag and gave it to Andy, who slipped it into his shirt pocket.

'Get warmed up there. Do your shadow-boxing. I'll go see what the story is.'

Maurice danced around the room throwing phantom combinations, monitoring his stance, body angled, guard tight, elbows protecting the ribs, chin tucked in, knuckles touching cheekbones.

Andy stuck his head in the door.

'You're on.'

Maurice followed him out into the hall and stood by the ringside, limbering up. The crowd consisted of other boxers and their families and friends, children running around, old lads wrapped up in overcoats, the back-row experts. Andy held the gloves open, big red and white 14 oz pillows. Once he was laced up, Maurice clambered onto the platform and slipped between the ropes. The canvas felt hard and unyielding through the thin soles of his boxing boots. The other boy, Breen, was already in the opposite corner, dancing on the spot. He had broad shoulders and thick legs and a ruddy farmer's face.

Andy rinsed the gumshield in the water bucket and popped it into Maurice's mouth. The feel of it against his palate always made him want to gag.

In through the nose, out through the mouth.

'Keep that chin tucked in,' Andy was saying. 'He's got reach, so try and get under his left and work inside.'

Maurice nodded, slapping his gloves together, bouncing on the balls of his feet. The ref climbed into the ring, a bald man in a white shirt. He called both boys together, barked out the rules and sent them back to their corners.

'Bring the fight to him,' Andy said, his voice charged with urgency. 'Good lad.'

The bell clanged. Maurice quickly crossed himself and moved to the centre of the canvas. The ref's hand was out in a suspended karate chop.

'Box!' he barked.

The two boys tapped gloves and began to circle each other. Maurice looked for an opening in the other boy's guard. He feinted a couple of left jabs, gauging Breen's reflexes, but something distracted him from getting stuck in.

Out the corner of his eye, he glimpsed a boy about his own age, standing slumped and slack-jawed in the neutral corner, gloved hands dangling limply round his knees, gumshield jutting out from his mouth like one of those Amazonian tribal faceplates. Drool ran down his chin.

A succession of hard jabs snapped Maurice's head back and then Breen was all over him. It felt like a wall falling in. A right hook to the gut left him winded and gasping for breath. His ears sang, shrill alarm bells jarred by the impact, his brain in scramble mode shrieking *fight-fight-fight* but all the connections were down, he couldn't get his guard up. He was dimly aware of Andy bellowing from the corner, instructing him to tighten up his guard.

A blow to the jaw sent Maurice's gumshield flying and his nose began to spout blood, blood running down the back of his neck like snot, spread all over his face and staining his singlet. The ref stopped the fight to retrieve the gumshield and handed it to Andy to rinse. Breen stood in the neutral corner. The apparition had vanished. The ref grabbed a towel and wiped blood from Maurice's face and instructed both boys to box on.

Breen came at him even wilder, throwing

haymakers, determined to finish the job. Maurice barely landed a punch. He threw his arms around the other boy's arms, trying to get his breath. His gloves were too heavy to lift, scalding tar in his veins. He couldn't breathe through the gumshield or see through the stinging sweat. They clung to each other like a pair of drunks trying to slowdance, then Breen disentangled himself and hemmed Maurice into a corner and unleashed a barrage of jabs and hooks and uppercuts.

The ref stopped the fight and sent Maurice to his corner.

He sat down hard on the stool and his chest heaved and burned as Andy held his head back and sponged blood from his face and said, *Good lad*, hushed as though in church. Maurice couldn't speak, all he could think of was that slow-eyed boy swaying on his feet in the neutral corner.

The referee beckoned both boys back to the centre of the ring and grasped their wrists. Maurice didn't even hear the verdict. All he could remember was the sinking feeling as the ref let go of his arm. He climbed down from the ring and hurried into the dressing room and sat slumped and dejected on the bench, trying to swallow the lump in his throat. Andy came in and undid the gloves.

'What happened, son?' he said.

Maurice couldn't answer.

He was quiet on the long drive home. The old man appeared at the back door when he got out of the car. Maurice shook his head and the crestfallen expression on his father's face was too much to bear, so he went straight to his room and lay on his bed, head splitting, the taste of blood in his mouth.

He could still taste it now, more than thirty years later. He put the book away and tried to recall the name of the boy who died in Balinbagin. He gazed into the swirling waters of the spit-sink beside the big green leather chair. There were traces of dried blood under the rim. He removed a packet of antibacterial wipes from one of the presses.

The boy's name was on the tip of his tongue. Something beginning with O.

He set about scrubbing away the stain.

On the way home I decided to take a look at the new African shop Jamey had mentioned. The market square buzzed with Friday afternoon shoppers, cars double-parked all over the place. I walked down Barracks Street, Jamey's envelope tucked under my arm. The shop wasn't hard to find. There was a stepladder splayed on a spattered tarpaulin in front of the main window display. A freshly painted sign hung over the door.

AFRO-KILCODY SUPERSTORES
Afro-Euro-Asian Goods

I stepped through the doorway. A dark-skinned man in a colourful shirt stood by the till talking to an old bloke in overalls. The shop swam with strange smells, paint and sawdust and the scorched scent of grain. A drill whined somewhere. There was a table set up near the back where a few young black men in football jerseys and baggy jeans sat around an ashtray, smoking and playing cards.

Under a handwritten sign, *Afro-Caribbean Foodstuffs*, there were labelled bags of maize and pounded yam, flour and goat meat, ground rice and bunches of coal-black bananas. There was a glass display stocked with videos with names like *Panumo* and *Gazula* and *Ayefele*. A rack of newspapers and magazines: *African Soccer*, *African Expatriate*, *Black Perspective*, *Nigerian Trumpet*. Brightly coloured bags and prints and batiks depicting tribal scenes. Displays of trinkets and medallions and ethnic jewellery. African drums. Sculptures and statuettes in the shapes of lions and elephants. Rastafarian coloured hats and scarves.

Ornamental letter openers shaped like knives, Easter Island faces carved in the handles.

The man on the counter cleared his throat.

'Can I help you?' he called over, in a pronounced accent.

I mumbled something about just browsing and hurried back out into the freakish heat.

The moon comes out from behind a cauliflower-shaped cloud, and its super-trouper lunar beam makes the crow glow, a tiny troll dandied up in top hat, spats and cane, ruffling his wings like jazz-hands and doing a tap dance on the road.

And he opens his beak and sings:

'Who's that a-writing?'

4

It was the bank holiday weekend and there was a disco on in the Rugby Club. Jamey was intent on celebrating the end of his exams and insisted I come along. I waited for him at the gate to the club grounds and watched the big moon glow over the fields until he finally swaggered down the road muttering excuses.

We fell into step with the other shadowy stragglers making the pilgrimage up the long drive toward the lights of the clubhouse. The bass signature of a song boomed and throbbed from the building, growing louder as we approached, drawing us to it like a homing signal.

'I should warn you, this place is a kip,' Jamey said. 'Rugger buggers and bogmen.'

The girl at the booth took our money and the cloakroom attendant tore tickets from a raffle roll, pinned them to the collars of our jackets and handed us the stubs and a couple of dinner vouchers. We stepped into the commotion and heat. Disco lights flashed and blinked and fragments of light refracted off the revolving mirror balls and swam around the walls like shoals of fishes. The music was irresponsibly loud, the air thick with beery smells and body odour and an underlay of piss and disinfectant.

'See if you can find us somewhere to sit,' Jamey yelled into my ear, then plunged into the bodies packed three deep at the bar.

The room was a split-level discothèque and lounge area. The mirrored walls were fogged with condensation and the floor sticky with spilled drink. UV light made specks of dandruff glow on people's clothes. Frugging bodies elbowed into each other. A balding man with hair grown long at the back and a woman in a yellow jumpsuit did the twist. A huge African-looking chap stood in front of the speakers, oblivious to the volume, surveying the floor like some rich rapper checking out the talent from behind a velvet rope. His skin was so black it was almost blue, shot-putter's shoulders and arms like legs and a barrel chest squeezed into a white T-shirt, hair cropped close to his head. Girls ogled him like they wanted to eat him up, and I couldn't help but feel a twinge of jealousy and awe.

I found a couple of grey stacking chairs and set them up at the edge of the dance floor. Jamey came back with a pint of beer in each hand and two more wedged between his forearms and ribs. He weaved carefully between tables laden with glasses filled to various levels, like receptacles left out for gathering rain, and carefully placed the drinks under our chairs.

The shirt was already stuck to the small of my back. I grabbed one of the glasses and gulped beer and grimaced at the bitter gassy taste and watched the dancers. A man in a swanky blazer-shirt-and-tie combo did a duck-walk. Jamey nodded at a big square-headed lump of a lad dressed in a shirt and slacks. Despite the heat, he had a jumper knotted around his neck. Car keys dangled from his belt loop like talismans for attracting girls. Jamey pumped his knee in time to the rhythms pounding from the sound system.

'What do you think of this music?' he shouted.

Some hyperactive dance track, repetitive beats, vocal speeded up.

'I told you, music's not really my thing.'

Jamey affected his sceptical look.

'For someone who claims he's not interested in music, you seem to pay very close attention to it.' He shook his head in lamentation. 'Sometimes I think you were dropped here in a Martian pod.'

Jamey was right, but I couldn't explain how I felt. Something about music seemed dangerous to me. It felt as though if I wasn't careful, it might overwhelm my senses, swallow me up.

Sunburned mountainy men slouched on the periphery of the floor, arms folded or hands thrust in their pockets, observing the action like sad silverbacks. Girls strutted and gyrated. Discombobulated lads tried to get their attention by mincing and face-making and throwing mock Travolta shapes. Jamey scrunched up his nose, obviously unimpressed by their moves.

'You ever notice how posh people can't dance?' he said.

I didn't answer. I'd always thought of Jamey's family as kind of posh.

There was a guy with crutches sitting on a corner bench. His right leg was in a cast and his face was pinched and coated in straggly red beard. A white singlet exposed wiry arms crudely tattooed with Indian ink, and he cradled a large bottle of Smithwicks between his thighs. Every so often he used one of his crutches to hike up dancers' skirts, and they recoiled and cursed at him.

I nudged Jamey.

'Who's the gimp?'

'Billy Dagg. Nasty piece of work.'

'What happened to his leg?'

'He got impudent one night upstairs in Donahue's.'

80

A sort of window hatch opened beside the bar, and within seconds a queue had formed.

Jamey handed me his meal ticket.

'Dinner is served,' he said. 'I got the drinks in.'

I was going to ask him why they served food this late, but didn't want to appear like more of a hick than I already was. Something to do with the licensing laws I figured. I lifted my pint and hurried across the floor to get in line for the hatch. The queue shuffled towards the window like convicts on a chain gang. Somebody jostled my elbow, spilling beer over my wrist and hand. I turned and saw the big African-looking bloke towering over me.

'Howya,' I said.

He nodded.

I wondered if any girls saw me talking to him, would they think I was his friend and ogle me too. We shuffled forward a bit more.

'So,' I said. 'Where you from anyway?'

He blanked me.

I made it to the front of the queue. The girl behind the hatch handed me napkins and plastic cutlery and two paper plates heaped with chicken and mashed potatoes. I ferried them back to our spot beside the dance floor and handed Jamey his plate.

The DJ, a gangly bloke with a '70s footballer haircut, interrupted the dance music to put on a slow song with a church organ melody. The floor cleared and just as quickly refilled with couples that began to dance close and kiss and grope each other's hair and backsides. The slow song gave way to a sort of melodramatic ballad with a really long saxophone solo. Jamey put his empty plate under the chair and wiped his mouth.

'John-boy,' he yelled into my ear, making it whine. 'Have you ever had a girl?'

'Say again?'

I had heard him fine.

'Have you ever, y'know, thrown the gob on anyone?'

'Not yet.'

'You're what age?'

'Fifteen.'

He looked at me sidelong and gestured around the room.

'We'll have to sort you out some cute Mercy bird. See anything you like?'

All the girls looked good to me, but there was one particularly pretty pale girl with red hair sitting with her friends at a table.

'Her.'

Jamey followed my line of sight.

'Oh man,' he said, 'you can pick 'em. That's Rachel Cullen.'

'She's nice.'

He grinned.

'It's all war paint. She slow-danced with me once one night and put her head right here' — he patted his shoulder — 'next morning I woke up and found the imprint of her face on my good shirt. It was like the Shroud of Turin.'

I felt the alcohol buzz kick in, that feeling of being surrounded by a force field, like I had the gift of temporary invincibility.

'I don't care,' I said. 'I'm going to ask her up.'

The girl's table was at the other side of the lounge. To get there I had to negotiate an assault course of chairs and tables and feet. The girl saw me coming and broke off from her conversation. She looked even better up close. Her friends stared like they expected me to make balloon animals or something.

'Would you like to dance?' I said, leaning across the table.

'What?' she yelled back.

Her friends exchanged glances and smirked and looked into their drinks.

'WOULD YOU — '

The music stopped.

' — LIKE TO DANCE?'

Rachel Cullen covered her mouth, and the friend to her left coughed *'freak'* into her fist.

'No thanks,' Rachel said. 'I'm with someone.'

The music restarted. I murmured something lame and beat a retreat. Jamey was
holding my pint out.

'Shot you down?'

I tried to act nonchalant.

'You were right. She didn't look that good
up close.'

Jamey put his arm around my shoulder and
leaned in, confidential.

'See what you did wrong there, though?'

Like I needed a post-mortem to prolong
the ordeal.

'You walked over there like you were
apologizing for being alive. Next time, put
your shoulders back and stick your chin out.
It's all attitude, man.'

'Nah,' I said, shaking my head. 'It's not
that. Girls just don't like me.'

Jamey flicked my ear.

'Don't be stupid. Course they do.'

'They don't. I've got a bad name around
the village.'

'Why?'

I drew in a deep breath. It was kind of
embarrassing, but I figured if he was my
friend, I could tell him.

'Well,' I said, 'this one time in school there
was a free class. Everyone was playing
spin-the-bottle. When the bottle pointed at
you, you had to tell some sort of secret. When

it came around to me, I didn't know what to say. I couldn't think of any secrets, so I made one up.'

'So what did you say?'

'I said I had a secret desire to stick it in a jar of worms.'

Jamey snorted.

'You're joking, man.'

I smiled a bit.

'Nope.'

'And did you?'

'Naw, I just wanted to shock them. It was all over the school in no time. All these Mercy girls kept coming up to me on the street and asking was it true. I just said yeah. It was easier than explaining.'

'Oh boy,' Jamey said. 'A jar of worms.'

The slow set ended. The DJ put on something loud and angry sounding, and couples dispersed like it was a fire drill. Blokes wearing cut-off denims charged the floor and played imaginary guitars and whipped their greasy hair in a rotary motion.

We drank our beers and Jamey got us a couple more. It was so hot I gulped it down, but didn't seem to be getting any drunker. The DJ played another slow set and one long fast one and then the national anthem. The lights came on and everyone stood except for Jamey, who sprawled in his chair, sipping the dregs of his pint and examining his fingernails. He noticed me staring.

'What?' he said. 'It's a crap song, man.'

Across the floor, Billy Dagg used his crutches to lever himself upright. He stood and glared at us.

'Jamey.'

'I see him. Relax.'

The national anthem ended in a clash of cymbals. Billy Dagg hobbled towards us, black eyes blazing. I stared, sort of transfixed, as he came closer and planted himself before Jamey.

'Better men than you died so that music could be played,' he said, 'and all you can do is sit on your hole and look smug, ya little cur.'

Jamey drained his glass and got up.

'C'mon, John,' he said.

We hurried into the hall and collected our jackets from the cloakroom and stepped out the front door, but Billy Dagg was blocking our way. Beer soured in my stomach. All the bouncers were inside routing the couples smooching in corners. We moved sideways, like we were trying to get past a wicked dog. I needed to pee really badly. Billy Dagg's fingers whitened on the grips of his crutches and his biceps bulged.

'Don't think I couldn't hammer the lard

out of both of you with the one hand,' he snarled, hobbling after us down the drive, the crutches making spazzy rhythms on the gravel.

Jamey stopped and turned.

'That'd hardly be a fair fight, Billy. We couldn't very well hit a cripple.'

Billy Dagg moved fast for a man on crutches. He balanced himself on one and swung the other at Jamey, who caught the rubber-castored butt between his hands and held tight. For a moment the two were locked in a bizarre tug o' war. Jamey called out to me, his voice calm.

'John, help me out here, man.'

I lunged for the other crutch and got a hold of it. Billy Dagg cursed and roared. It was ridiculous.

'Count of three,' Jamey yelled. *'Three!'*

He wrenched on his crutch and I wrenched on mine and we jerked backwards like we'd pulled apart a huge Christmas cracker. Billy Dagg wobbled a bit and fell onto his front. He began to claw at the gravel, ranting and foaming at the mouth as he tried to get to his feet.

We legged it down the drive, ran until we lost ourselves in the warm night, darkness like soot on our skin, sweating and sobered with fright, running until our chests burned and we had to stop to catch our breath.

Jamey bent, hands on his kneecaps. He was wheezing like an old man.

'Stitch,' he gasped. 'I need a rest. Got any smokes?'

I checked the packet.

'Just the one.'

We passed the cigarette back and forth. Jamey considered the last few smoke-able millimetres.

'Leave us a scald,' I said.

He shook his head.

'We'll split it.' He considered the tapered red tip of the fag and carefully tapped off the ash. 'Open your gob.'

'What for?'

'Just open up.'

He dragged deep on the cigarette, flicked it away, grabbed my head and clamped his mouth onto mine and hawed smoke down my throat. Then he put his fingers under my chin and pushed my gawping mouth closed.

I doubled up coughing, smoke coming out of every hole in my head.

'For future reference,' Jamey said, 'that's a blowback.'

He set off down the road.

We walked through the new estates that had sprouted on the outskirts of the village, gravelled driveways and neatly mowed lawns and security lights that winked on as we approached and flicked off after we'd passed. Soon the houses began to look like clapboard replicas of themselves. Above us, young summer stars glimmered in an inexplicable sky.

'I'm starving again,' Jamey said. 'Must be the adrenalin.'

'Or else you've got worms.'

Jamey rolled his eyes.

'We could get something at my place,' I said. 'Maybe some toast.'

'I'd murder some toast. How far?'

'Ten, fifteen minutes.'

On we went until the houses thinned out and there were no more lights. We trudged through the soft night until we came across a dead bird lying on the grass verge. Jamey stooped to get a better look. It was an owl. There was sticky-looking blood all over its wings and its huge creepy-toy eyes were closed. It had the purest, whitest feathers I'd ever seen.

'Jesus,' Jamey said, and shook his head.

We walked the last couple of hundred yards to my house. I took the key from under the flower pot on the step and let us in. Jamey sat at the kitchen table while I put the kettle on and made toast and removed plates from the cupboard with the exaggerated care of a burglar.

'This is the best fuckin' thing I ever tasted,' Jamey said, spewing crumbs everywhere.

There were footfalls upstairs, directly over the kitchen.

'Shit,' I said. 'She's up.'

Boots came down the stairs. My mother appeared in the kitchen doorway, fully dressed and wide awake. She was always a light sleeper.

'Ma,' I said brightly.

She took in the scene.

'Who's this boy?'

Jamey got to his feet and took my mother's hand.

'Jamey Corboy, ma'am. So sorry we woke you.'

She seemed a bit taken aback. So was I. The manners on him.

'It's all right, I was getting up anyway.'

My mother plugged in the kettle.

'You lads must be hungry.'

Jamey looked at me, eyebrow raised, as my mother got out the frying pan and a bottle of sunflower oil and lit the cooker. She cracked a couple of eggs into the pan and put more bread in the toaster.

'So, Mrs D,' Jamey said, his voice raised over the crackling of the pan.

'*Mrs D?*' I mouthed at him.

My mother shovelled the eggs with a spatula.

'Yes, Jamey.'

'You look far too young to be John's mother. You must have had him very young.'

My mother flipped the eggs, swirled the oil around, flipped them again.

'Oh, I had him when I was meant to, not before. John, set the table for us, will you, son?'

I got out the cutlery, avoiding my mother's eyes. She dished up the food and sat nursing a cup of tea while we ate.

'How are your mother and father, Jamey?' she said.

'Fine, thanks.'

He was trying to simultaneously wolf down eggs and not speak with his mouth full.

'And your brother?'

'Good form. Bit of a handful.'

'You're fond of him, though.'

Jamey half smiled.

'Hard not to be.'

I watched this exchange like a spectator at a tennis match. My mother took a sip of her tea.

'He's going to the special school, is that right?'

'He is.'

'And he's getting on well?'

'Loves it.'

'That's good. More eggs?'

91

'No thanks, I'm full as a tick.'

He laid his knife and fork on the plate and patted his stomach.

'Mrs D, they named you well.'

'How so?'

'That was divine.'

She smothered a smile.

'Don't be soft-soaping me, you. Smoke?'

She picked up her box of Silk Cut Blue and offered him one. I couldn't believe what I was seeing.

'I shouldn't, Mrs D, but thanks very much.'

They sat puffing away like old friends, and when Jamey finished his cigarette, my mother said, 'You'd better get home now, son. Your mother and father will be worried if they wake up and you're not there.'

Jamey nodded and pushed his chair back.

'You're right, Mrs D. I'll go.'

He clasped my mother's hand between both of his and looked her in the eye.

'Pleasure meeting you.'

'And you.'

He turned to me.

'John, would you walk me up the road a bit so I can get my bearings?'

I glanced at my mother. She was looking at him thoughtfully.

'Ma? Is that OK?'

She almost jumped.

'Fine, fine. Come straight back though. You need to get to bed or you'll be no good to me tomorrow.'

We ducked out the front door and walked briskly up the road. Cows stood motionless in the fields like topiary shapes. Jamey cleared his throat.

'That was weird,' he said.

'She was really giving you the eyeball.'

'I noticed. Trying to get my measure. She thinks the sun shines out of your fundament.'

'Come off it.'

'She does. Only-child syndrome. Wait until you try and leave home. That's when the fireworks'll start.'

He stopped walking and looked around at the fields with the bemusement of a born townie.

'I think I can find my way from here. You'd better go back.'

I watched until he was obscured by a hump in the road. I could still feel the effects of the drink and smoke swirling in my lungs, my bloodstream, my brain. The backs of my eyeballs ached as I stared up at the heavens, the long dead stars, and when I shut my eyes the after-light remained imprinted on my mind, lotus-shaped lights flowering into big white wows.

I hoped Jamey's parents were heavy sleepers.

It'd be morning soon.

Shapes stirred in the shadows of my room. A skull-faced crone with parchment skin who unfolded her withered briar limbs and moved to the foot of my bed. Nails long as thorns clawed back the bedspread. I couldn't move. Cold crawled all over my skin, arousing thousands of tiny nipples. The crone pawed my legs with gnarled fingers, witch-teats grazing my balls and belly and chest. The smell of her breath, her hideous face, her mouth clamped on mine, the stink, the suffocating tongue down my throat scooping the air from my lungs.

When I woke, the too-sweet reek of old-lady perfume filled my nostrils. It smelled like fly-spray, overripe fruit. I crept onto the landing and sat on the top step and listened. Downstairs in the kitchen, tea gurgled from the pot and cups clattered on saucers. I needed to go to the bathroom but couldn't resist eavesdropping for a bit.

'They're taking over the country, Lily,' Mrs Nagle was saying. 'Look at the Methodist church above in Ballycarn.'

Mrs Nagle and my mother appeared to have patched up their differences and now she was a regular visitor again. It started tentatively enough, with a shout over the ditch, or a salute on the road as she passed, then she'd ask to use the phone or have a look at the paper, squinting at the headlines in a manner that suggested she harboured a deep distrust of the written word.

She usually appeared when we were sitting down to eat. My mother reckoned the smell of cooking drew her out of her lair. She always had some comment to make about how many stone I'd lost and wasn't I gone fierce anguished-looking, the flesh falling off my bones. My mother took no notice, just gave me the odd wink behind her back.

Mrs Nagle slurped her tea and made an *aaaah* sound.

'Used to be there wasn't a sinner in it of a Sunday,' she said, 'the quietest little country chapel. Now you wouldn't find a seat. Mrs Tector from beyond in the Holla was giving out, she says you can hardly get in the door of a Sunday with their singing and banging tambourines and all this happy-clappy business. If we're not careful, they'll start the same carry-on here. God knows it's bad enough as it is, what with all these fecken folk masses.'

My mother cleared her throat. I could almost hear her smirk.

'It's not the same since they did away with the Latin, Phyllis.'

'Never mind that. These crowd are worse than the boat people ever were.'

The tap ran.

'Hah, Lily?' she demanded. 'Isn't that right?'

Mrs Nagle couldn't bear to think she wasn't being agreed with, but my mother wouldn't be drawn, so she changed tack.

'I see John's gotten great with that young Corboy,' she said. 'His mother's a pretty little thing. If a bit . . . affected.'

Now I was all ears. I stole down the steps, taking care to avoid the creaky one.

'Aye,' said my mother.

Mrs Nagle took my mother's reluctance to elaborate as a signal to continue.

'He's a quare card, that youngster. I wonder if he isn't a bit of a sissy.'

'That's enough now, Phyllis.'

'You can't be too careful raring a young lad these days is all I'm saying. Things are not like they were in our time.'

There was a lapse in the conversation, and the air seemed to almost quiver with what was unspoken. Then Mrs Nagle said, 'How's John been in himself lately?'

'He's fine.'

'Y'know, there was talk around the village about the pair of them.'

'People always talk, Phyllis. It's what they do when they've nothing better to occupy themselves with. You know that.'

'Aye, well, I hope that little louser didn't corrupt your John . . . '

'Phyllis — '

' . . . Turn him into a molly boy or anything.'

A hand slapped the table, causing the cups and saucers to rattle.

'That's enough of that kind of talk, Phyllis. Whoever my son chooses to knock about with is his own business.'

'Ah here, Lily . . . '

'I'm telling you. Be on your way. I've had my fill of you for one morning.'

A chair scraped.

'All right,' Mrs Nagle said. 'If you can't be civil with me, you can keep your own company. God knows you're used to it.'

She hurried into the hall and caught sight of me on the stairs. Her eyes narrowed into slits. She hurried out and slammed the door. My mother put the latch on and did a double-take when she spotted me on the step.

'Did you hear any of that?' she said.

I shrugged my shoulders.

'Couldn't help but.'

She rolled her eyes.

'Pay no attention. Mrs Nagle says more than her prayers.'

Old Crow sleeps like a bat, hanging upside down by his claws from the withered bough of a dead alder tree, and as he sleeps he dreams, and what he dreams of is a thousand years ago, when a rabble drunk on mead plundered Clonmacnoise, and for their sins were stricken with a plague that laid waste to the county. Snow covered everything, cold caused the perishing of fowl and fish and wild animals. Lightning struck, crops were blighted and there followed a great earthquake; a fiery steeple appeared in the air for five hours, and out of it emerged flocks of black birds that picked up a greyhound from the middle of a town and carried it away, and in their wake there came the worst of all murrains.

5

Chapel bells pealed through the Sunday morning peace, calling the people of Kilcody out to Mass. Jamey and his family sauntered up the road like a troupe of weird birds, Maurice first, a tall man with a receding hairline and thin body, except for a bulbous paunch that put the buttons of his white sleeve-rolled shirt under pressure. Dee followed a half-step behind dressed in a sort of trouser suit, her tired blond hair loosened about her shoulders. As for Jamey, he was an eye-opener in his blah-coloured slacks, hair slicked back from his face with some sort of oily gunk, holding Ollie's hand. They crunched across the pebbles, Dee sort of shooing the boys inside while trying to keep abreast of her husband.

Jamey stopped to scrutinise the coloured stones arrayed across one side of the path. He peered a bit, lip-synced what they spelled out —

MERDE A DIEU

— and a grin split his face. Dee snapped at him to hurry on, so he scrambled the pebbles with his shoe and tramped into the chapel, where hymn-singers had already started to hail the queen of heaven.

I was watching from among the head-stones, hunkered under the great granite archangel, chuckling to myself. A shadow fell across the stone.

'I'm watching you.'

Mrs Nagle loomed, ten feet tall. Her feet seemed to hover clear inches over the grass, and her finger was extended, the nail overgrown and twisted like a briar. She retracted her arm and receded from me, taking her shadow with her, moving back-wards as if on wires, an optical trick, before gliding through the chapel's open mouth.

'Who said Mass?' my mother asked when she heard me come in.

'Father Quinn.'

'Did he preach?'

'For about a week.'

'What was he saying?'

'Something about life being like a mini-marathon. Couldn't make out the half of it. That man talks like he has a toothache.'

'That priest. Not that man.'

'Is a priest not a man?'

She considered answering, thought the better of it.

'Don't be a smart alec.'

Ever since her operation my mother tried to quit the fags every few months, but the cravings always got the better of her. Her mood got worse each day she was off them, and didn't improve a whole lot when she relapsed. I made for the stairs.

'Hold on. Sit down here a second.'

Reluctantly I pulled out a chair as my mother jerked the table drawer open, removed a book and sent it skidding across the surface.

'I found that in your room.'

I looked at the book. It was only *Harper's Compendium*.

'What's the big deal?' I said. 'I've had that for years.'

She took out a cigarette, tapped it against the box and jabbed it in the direction of the book.

'I know, and I don't want you reading it any more. You're a young man nearly and you've still got worms on the brain. It can't be good.'

'You're not serious.'

'I am.'

I made a grab for the book, but my mother was quicker. She snatched it from my fingertips and let me have it across the jaw.

I yelped, more surprised than hurt.

'What was that for?'

'Impudence, that's what.'

Smoke trailed from her fag-hand as she crossed the room and picked up the Bible from under her armchair and slapped it on the table before me.

'You'd be better off reading this.'

I grabbed the wireless from off the kitchen counter and stormed out of the kitchen.

'It wouldn't do you any harm,' she yelled after me as I stomped upstairs to my bedroom. I turned the radio on so loud the loose bits rattled. The racket soon brought my mother upstairs, the door flying open, her face making a face. Her eyes roamed over the stacks of books, the heaped comics, the sheaves of papers and drawings, and she shook her head, as though denying permission for something I hadn't asked for.

'You need to tidy up this room,' she yelled over the blaring radio. 'It's a *disaster.*'

She shut the door and her boots thumped down the steps. Soon after that, the front door slammed.

When I'd cooled off a bit I sloped downstairs. The Bible was where she'd left it on the table. I made a bread-and-butter sandwich and a cup of tea and used it as a tray and crept back up to my room. Belly down on the bed, I opened the Bible at random. Words glowed from the page.

'*How much less man, that is a worm? And the son of man, which is a worm?*'

Over the next few days I repeatedly asked my mother what she'd done with my book. Eventually she admitted to throwing it out. I stormed from the house and stalked off into the village. I made enquiries at the library to see if they could find me a copy, but when the librarian went through her files, she could find no record of such a book. It was as though it never existed.

Outside, tarmac bubbled and blistered on the road. The ground was so hot I could feel it radiating through the rubber soles of my runners. I set off for the dump on the outskirts of the village, a good half-hour's hike. I'd decided to comb through the rubbish for *Harper's Compendium*. The odds against finding it were a million to one or worse, but that wasn't really the point. The point was to satisfy myself that it was gone for good.

The sun beat down on stubbled yellow fields. The earth was shorn of its blond hair, and the hay was gathered in bales the size of wagon wheels. By the time I got to the dump I was lathered in sweat. All afternoon I combed through heaps of refuse. I rooted through PVC sacks full of rotten food and dirty nappies and Styrofoam cups. I sifted mounds of sun-bleached newspapers, broken radios and VCRs and ribbons of videotape. I sorted through sad rain-spoiled soft toys, cracked plastic fish tanks, rotten rabbit hutches carpeted with pellets, big bulging sacks the shape of really fat people. By the time the sun had begun to set I was dog-tired and thirsty and my arms and legs ached.

The highest mound of muck afforded a panoramic view of the surrounding landfill and the bare fields beyond. The holy light of sunset transformed the dump into a glittering city of worship, mosques and cathedrals and citadels of junk, congregations of rats and cats and seagulls. It no longer mattered that the book was lost. I'd read it so often I could remember reams of it by heart. Probably could have recited the sections on parasites from memory. I sat lotus-legged atop the pyramid imagining I was some kind of Zen master or warrior monk. A seagull circled overhead, wingtips describing mystical whorls and spirals in the burnt-orange sky.

I drew a deep breath, located the centre of myself and called out to the gull.

'For every self-sufficient creature on earth,' I said, 'there are four parasites. 1.4 out of 6 billion people have roundworm. 1 billion have whipworm. 1.3 billion are infected with hookworms. Fourteen different kinds of parasites can live in the bowels of a duck.'

I rose to my feet and gestured at the sprawling topography of rubbish, and again called out to the wheeling, showboating gull.

'The tapeworm is a flat creature with no mouth or eyes that lives in the intestines,' I said. 'It can lay up to a million eggs a day and grows up to sixty feet long. He — or she — is made up of thousands of segments, each with its own male and female organs. Having no mouth or stomach, the tapeworm absorbs food through millions of gills.'

My chest swelled and my eyes rolled over the landfill, taking in the banjaxed washing-machines and ratty armchairs, the collapsed cardboard boxes and broken umbrellas and discarded items of clothing. Shoes. Lots of shoes, estranged from their former partners, gone downhill since the separation, laces frayed, tongues showing. A duvet stained with the shapes of countries that never existed. Bursted pillows, feathers everywhere. Used condoms, bodily fluids curdled in rubber nipples.

'*Toxoplasma gondii*,' I said, 'otherwise known as eggs in cat shit, can cause fatal brain damage in foetuses. Rats tested with *Toxoplasma* have been shown to become reckless to the point of being a danger to themselves. Some people reckon the same affliction makes human males feckless, women highly sociable and accommodating.'

I took another breath and spewed out facts like a human computer.

'Tanbura's guinea worms grow to two feet long and escape the body by crawling out through blisters. Threadworms live in the large intestine and the rectum, laying eggs at night. When you scratch your butt in your sleep, the eggs get under your nails, into your mouth, down the hatch, hatch, and the whole cycle starts again.'

All across the dump were scattered reams of wasted paper, bills, brochures, fast-food coupons, offers of credit cards, debt-consolidation plans.

'If you eat and eat,' I said, 'but you can't seem to get full, that's probably a parasite stealing all the good from your food intake. This is how parasites make people under-weight and cause drooling, bedwetting, insomnia and teeth-grinding. Itching in the ears, nose and assorted other cracks and crevices. How they make people go to the toilet too little or too much. How they turn your skin yellow and cause mucus problems and spots and headaches and bloody stools. Impotence. Gas. Fatigue. Depression. Baldness. Stupidity.'

Rats rustled. Gulls shrieked. Somewhere in

the distance, the looped *bow-wow-wow* of a dog. And the drone of an engine, coming closer.

I squinted across the fields. The sound of the engine swelled. A white hi-ace van bumped down the grass-split lane and came to a stop just inside the gates. A man got out and began to rummage through the multicoloured mounds. He had on baggy slacks belted with nylon tights, belly bulging out of a short-sleeved shirt decorated with dice and death's heads and fiery writing that said: *ROLL THEM BONES.*

It was Har Farrell. I hadn't seen him since my tenth birthday, when he gave me the crossbow. He was five years older now, must have been pushing fifty, and he'd put on a fair bit of weight since. My mother said he'd been away to England for a while, and when he came back he'd given up the drink and was a whole new person. He traded in the Honda 50 and bought a van and moved into the video business — blueys according to gossip — then diversified into bootleg designer knock-offs, bulk orders of duty-free, black-market stuff.

I watched him poke through the spare tyres and broken household appliances. He must have sensed he was being spied on, because he stopped foraging and stuck his head up like a meerkat. When he saw me, he crossed himself.

'Sweet Jesus,' he said. 'You gave me a scare there, young fella.'

His bushy hair was damp. He was pumping sweat.

'You're like a little green genie up there,' he said. 'All you're missing is the fecken hookah. Come down here and not have me shouting.'

I scrambled down from the mound and grinned.

'Hello, Har,' I said.

'Good god!' He took a step back. 'John Devine! You're after stretching a bit. Last time I set eyes on you, you weren't as big as a god's cow. How's your mother, son? I haven't seen her this donkey's years. Not since I took that television set off her hands. You were still only a scut.' His bulging shirt shook with suppressed chuckles. Chewing gum poked out the side of his mouth like a crooked tooth. 'By god, you weren't too pleased about it.'

'I remember.' I reached into my jacket pocket for my cigarettes. 'Smoke?'

He took another half-step back and held his hand out like he was stopping traffic.

'Gave 'em up,' he said. 'The pipes are bad. Any sense, you'll do the same. Bastard hard, though. Constipated for a month. Got piles on me arse like grapes. But I managed to keep my figure.'

He tugged at the tights around his waist.

'What brings you here?' I said.

'Oh, just looking for bits and bobs. This place is a goldmine usually. Want to buy a phone?'

'No thanks. Those things turn your brain to black pudding.'

'Ah.' He made a scoffing noise. 'That's your mother talking.'

He spat his gum into some silver paper, put it back in his shirt pocket, and with a flourish, produced a card and gave it to me.

Harry Farrell
Miscellaneous Goods
'If we can't get it, it can't be got.'

'You need anything son, anything at all, the number's on the back.'

He moved the briefcase onto the passenger side, grabbed hold of the steering wheel and hauled himself into the van.

'Tell your mother I was asking for her.'

He started the engine. I watched him drive away through the perimeter of rusting car hulks and patches of yellowed grass like crime-scene outlines testifying to recent acts of autocide, and then he was gone.

I walked home across the meadows, cutting through a three-cornered field with an old fairy fort in the middle, a stand of evergreens encircled by a wall built from quarry stones. The grass there was long and yellowed. I was exhausted by the day's toil, so I lay down to rest in the shade of the fort. I gazed at the reddening sky, and after a while I could scarcely tell if I was lying flat on the face of the earth or hanging from its underside, magnetised by gravity. I closed my eyes, but the skin of my eyelids didn't so much blot out the twilight sun as merely dim its intensity. My mind wandered, drugged with heat and fatigue, imagining the world as a stone skimming across the surface of space, sending ripples outward across the universe. Or maybe it was a ball bobbing in the vast blueness. A mote of dust floating across the pollen-strewn heavens.

A rustling sound made me open my eyes and sit up, dizzy and confused. When the sunspots cleared, I saw a grey buck hare, not ten yards away. He watched me warily before burrowing into a hole under the wall of the fairy fort. Slow and stealthy, I got to my feet and crept after him in a sort of caveman's crouch, and I climbed over the wall and into the shadowy glade.

The air was rich with pine-needle smells.

Cones were scattered on the ground like grenades. It was dank and cool, sheltered by a latticework of overhanging branches. I pushed through the leaves and came to a clearing at the centre of the fort, where the ground rose steeply into a clay mound.

Suddenly cold, I rubbed my arms.

At the summit of the mound was a nest of briars and twigs. I climbed the slope to get a better look. Inside the nest, a single black egg lay on a bed of black feathers. As I ran my fingers over its smooth surface, a jagged line began to work its way across the shell with a wet cracking sound. The egg broke apart and I caught a glimpse of blood-smeared flesh, a single eye, inflamed and rheumy, and I drew back and lost my footing and slipped and tumbled down the slope. Above me, something cawed and screeched. I scrambled to my feet and bolted, headlong through the thicket, thorns and briars scratching my skin, clothes smeared and torn. Hoofs thudded the ground behind me, hot breath on my neck. I cleared the wall and tore across the field, black wings rending the air at my back.

Spears of light seared through my eyelids. I opened them. My shirt was sodden with sweat and I was weakened by the heat. Above me, the dying sun glared down, a bloodshot Cyclops eye.

~

School was out long enough for the novelty to have worn off. The radio kept saying it was the warmest summer in years, that burn-time was down to an all-time low of twenty minutes. Everywhere felt central heated.

Slathered in my mother's sun cream, I met with Jamey outside Donahue's pub. He was slouched against the wall as though posing for a photograph, one boot flat against terracotta brickwork tagged with faded Tippex swastikas and Crass logos and H-Block slogans.

'You gonna help me spend this?' he said, waving a wad of notes.

Earlier that day his family had left on holiday, entrusting him with the keys to the house. Dee was nervous, and when his dad's back was turned she slipped him a handful of twenties 'for emergencies'.

'I've to meet someone inside,' Jamey said. 'Have a pint with me while I'm waiting. I'm buying.'

We ducked into the pub. The dank shade and stale beer smells were a welcome relief from the blazing sunlight. A television blared over the bar. To the rear of the room, on a small stage set into an alcove that looked like a midget Santa's grotto, a man in a short-sleeved summer shirt plugged a mandolin into a buzzing Peavey amp. He fiddled with a crackling lead and ran a plectrum over the strings. The chord rang out, almost medieval-sounding. Satisfied, he turned the amp off, killing the hum, and nipped out to the beer garden for a smoke.

Jamey brought two pints over to the corner snug and set them on the table.

'Who you meeting?' I said.

'Gunter Prunty. Biker type. Works in Waxon. Remember I told you about the fags and booze I ripped off from The Ginnet? His idea.'

I never understood why Jamey got involved in this kind of stuff. He was capable of doing the dumbest things.

'I kept lookout while he went in the skylight,' he said. 'Gunter cut me in.'

We were just getting stuck into our second round when the main door opened. Sunshine flooded the room and backlit three tall men in wax jackets and heavy boots. The biggest of them wore elaborate sideburns and a goatee and had an oversized head like a St Bernard's. His hair was done in a sort of greaser pompadour, tapering off in an aerodynamic spoiler at the collar.

'Speak of the devil,' Jamey said under his breath.

Gunter strode over to the bar and put his elbows on the counter and his right boot on the foot rail. He was well over six feet tall. As though sensing he was being stared at, he scanned the room. His eyes stopped at our table. Jamey raised his glass and dipped his head. Gunter nodded back. His friends climbed onto the high stools.

'The one with the ponytail is Fintan,' Jamey said, barely moving his lips. 'He works in the glass factory in Ballo. The ferrety-looking lad in the denim jacket is Davy. Acid casualty. Scrambled his medulla oblongata.'

Gunter bought a pint of stout and took a gulp. He hitched up his baggy-arsed jeans and lurched towards our table. He moved like a man who'd spent time inventing a whole new way of walking. You could feel the impact of his motorcycle boots as they clodded off the wooden floorboards.

Jamey slid over in the seat.

'Boys,' Gunter said, and put his stout on the table. 'Mind if we join you?'

He beckoned the other two over without waiting for an answer.

The musician came in from the beer garden, strapped on his mandolin and plucked out a melody. He closed his eyes, put his lips to the microphone and began to sing in a nasal, reedy voice rendered metallic by the dinky PA.

'*Well, the cuckoo,*' he whinnied, '*she's a pretty bird, and she wobbles as she flies.*'

We all huddled in the snug like shaggy beasts. It was hard to hold a conversation, so we watched the singer until he took another break. Gunter bought us a round. He removed a match from between his teeth as one of the bar girls set the drinks down.

'So, Jay,' he said. 'You still writing them yarns?'

'On and off.'

'Tell us one.'

'What, now?'

'Aye. No such thing as a free drink, ever hear that said?'

I could imagine the conflict in Jamey's mind. He wouldn't appreciate being talked at like he was a performing monkey. But at the same time, he loved the attention.

'Ever hear the one about Philip Divilly?' he said after a few moments' consideration.

Gunter gulped from his glass.

'I did not,' he said, wiping foam from his lip. 'Tell me.'

Jamey cleared his throat.

'About fifty years ago, Philip Divilly was considered the finest tenor in the whole county. The sound of his airs used to put people in a trance. Women fell in love with him on the spot.'

Fintan raised his head and glowered, a dog disturbed from its thoughts.

'Pishróg,' he muttered.

'Go on, son,' Gunter said to Jamey. 'Don't mind him.'

'Well,' Jamey continued, 'the men of Balinbagin didn't like that one bit. So they got together and went to see an old tinker witch famous for curing warts and shingles and shit. Long story short, they asked her would she put a hex on him.'

Fintan tightened his ponytail and yawned.

'Pish,' he said, 'róg.'

'Shut your cake-hole, Fin,' Gunter snapped.

Jamey ignored the interruption and continued with the story.

'She refused at first,' he said, 'but they kept driving up the price until she couldn't refuse any longer and she went to work with her rabbits' feet and bowls of milk and eye of newt and toe of frog and all that jive.'

Jamey's voice grew louder, gaining confidence in the story. His speech patterns had begun to mimic Gunter's gruff tones, and I wondered if Gunter noticed.

'One morning Philip Divilly woke up and his voice was gone. All the boys of Balinbagin were delighted. But they made a bad mistake.

When it came time to pay the witch, they reneged on the deal and offered her half what they'd agreed on. She told them to shove their money and sought out Philip Divilly. She told him about how all the men of Balinbagin were set again him. Well, he went apeshit. He vowed revenge, and the witch was only too glad to help. She told him that come the next full moon, he was to stand on the crossroads and at the stroke of midnight begin to sing. Didn't matter what, so long as he opened his mouth.

'So he went out to the crossroads and when midnight struck he drew in an almighty breath and let it out and a great wind rose up and sparks flew around him like a bonfire, and a spirit flew into his gob and he was changed from a man into a sort of wraith.'

'What's a wraith?' Gunter said.

'A demon. Y'know, like a ring-wraith. His face grew long and a goat's smeg grew on his chin and he stretched to twelve feet tall and he looked a right mad bastard.'

'A bit like Fintan here,' Gunter said, and planted a slow-motion punch on his friend's jaw. Fintan affected a horrible parody of a grin that vanished from his face as quickly as it appeared. Jamey went on talking, his voice as portentous as a preacher's.

'So he wreaked a terrible vengeance on the

men of Balinbagin. He broke into their houses while they slept and slit their throats and pulled out their tongues and ate their hearts and drank their blood.'

He paused for breath and a sip of his drink and then continued.

'He still walks the roads at night, and anyone who hears his voice is lulled asleep. And he takes out a slash-hook blade and slits their throat and puts his mouth to the wound and sucks their soul out through their windpipe. And he keeps those souls in his pocket and sells one to Old Nick every Halloween in exchange for another year on earth.

'They say if you put your ear to the ground any summer's night you can hear his boots on the road no matter where he is in the county, and the only protection from him is to sing at the top of your voice so you can't hear his magic airs.'

Jamey took another slurp of his beer, sat back and folded his arms.

'Is that it?' Gunter said.

'That's it.'

The musician in the corner started tuning up his mandolin for another song.

Gunter said, 'How come you never spin yarns like that, Fintan?'

Fintan shrugged and said, 'You ever hear

the one about Snow White and Pinocchio?'

'I think I've been spared that one,' Gunter said.

'Aye,' Fintan continued. 'Snow White is sitting on Pinocchio's face moaning tell-a-lie-tell-the-truth-tell-a-lie-tell-the-truth.'

Gunter cackled and threw more stout down his throat.

There was a bad feeling in the room, squalid and muggy. Somehow, the beer had soured in my mouth. Dust motes danced in the shafts of window light; everything had taken on an amber cast. I got to my feet.

'What's up?' Gunter said. 'The company not to your liking?'

'I may go,' I said. 'I'll see you later, Jamey.'

Jamey nodded, but wouldn't meet my eye, only a quick sidelong glance, as if I'd seen something I wasn't supposed to see.

'Later,' was all he'd say.

A harvest moon rose in the mackerel sky as I walked home, alcohol buzzing in my head like background radiation.

My mother was sat at the kitchen table. Before her was a bottle of Powers, a glass and a Silk Cut Blue burning in the seashell ashtray. A tallow candle gouted in a saucer, its aquarium light playing across her face.

'Your dinner's in the oven,' she said, her

speech slow and deliberate. I hung my jacket on the back of a chair.

'You all right?'

Something flickered in her eyes. I couldn't read its meaning. She rubbed her face.

'I was at the doctor's for a check-up.'

'How'd that go?'

She looked away.

'The usual. Give up the fags. Eat more fruit.'

I dipped my chin, indicating the bottle.

'Thought you were a Pioneer.'

'I was. I recovered.'

She took a mouthful from her glass and coughed.

'Have one with me, why don't you?'

Her chair scraped the floor as she got up and took a glass from the draining board and tipped whiskey into it. She placed the drink before me like a dare.

'Go on,' she said. 'Don't tell me you never broke your pledge. I can smell the beer off you from here.'

I accepted the glass and took a sip, aware of her eyes on me. Uncharted territory. Whiskey burned all the way down to my stomach. She offered me one of her cigarettes. Again I wavered.

'Oh take one ower that,' she snapped. 'And sit down for heaven's sake. You're making me nervous standing there.'

I held my hair back from the candle's flame and lit the cigarette. My mother gazed out the window and contemplated whatever was out there for a few moments. When she spoke again her voice had softened.

'I was just thinking about when I first went travelling.'

I took a chair and sipped the whiskey. I liked the warm feeling in my stomach, harsh but somewhat comforting. Candle shadows threw ju-jitsu shapes on the walls.

'Where?' I said.

'England. Scotland. I was following a man.'

I looked at the table, a bit embarrassed. She took a drag of smoke and chortled through her nose.

'A musician, of all things,' She shook her head, close to smiling. 'We met at one of the demonstrations they used to have at Ballo harbour when they were going to build a power plant or something down there. It was a kind of festival.'

The way she spoke was like I wasn't there. She gazed out at the dim shadows of the trees.

'His band was camped out down the prom that night,' she said. 'They sat up all hours round a fire playing music like a bunch of gypos. I stayed listening until the sun came up. I got into trouble for being out so late, but I didn't care. I was a grown woman. My brothers left me to stop home and mind our mother and father, like an old spinster. But that night put a longing on me. There must have been a bit of tinker in my blood. The night before they were due to go back to England, they asked me to come away with them. I said I would. I'd never been out of the county in my life.'

'And did you?'

'I did, faith.'

She looked at the window again, as if reading something in the condensation there.

'We travelled all over England that summer. When we had a bit of money we stayed in B&Bs. If we were stuck, we'd all bunk down in the van, sleeping on big squares of foam rubber. Or if the weather was fine, we camped out.'

She paused to lift the bottle and top up our glasses, dribbling some on the table. She wiped the spillage with the sleeve of her cardigan.

'They were some crowd, all right. Only young lads. The curse of being happy, John, is you never realise it at the time. As soon as you do, it's over.'

She swirled the glass, as though trying to decipher the liquid's quiddity, and knocked back a mouthful like it was water.

'Come the end of the summer, we drove all the way up to the highlands. His people owned a bit of a farm near this little village in the Northeast. He came from money I think.'

'What was his name?'

'Never you mind.'

She looked out from under her eyebrows and hefted a sigh.

'You were named after an old hymn he taught me. You wouldn't sleep as a baby. One night there was a storm warning on the radio, and I got frightened, and I sang to comfort you.'

'What was the song?'

'John the Revelator.'

She took a sip of whiskey, her face a scowl of concentration. And she began to sing.

'*Who's that a-writing? John the Revelator.*'

Her voice was throaty and hoarse, but strong.

'*John the Revelator wrote the book of the seven seals.*'

She wiped her mouth with her sleeve and took a drink.

'It worked,' she said. 'It sent you off to sleep. So I named you John.'

She stubbed out her cigarette in the overflowing ashtray.

'The plan was to set up camp in the farmhouse and make a record of his songs. He was handy with the equipment. Used to take amplifiers apart and put them back together again using nothing but pliers and a soldering iron and a roll of sticky tape.'

She shook a fresh cigarette from the box and lit it.

'We travelled through the hilly country. Nothing only mountains and forests and whiskey distilleries. It was very near the coast. He said it was a holy place and in the old days people settled there because of the soil. The land was more fertile than any other part of the country. The cabbages were famous, big as bushes.

'It was still bright at ten o'clock the night we arrived. The farm looked like the last place God made. There was a long lane from the main road up to a big stone house and a few barns and a haggart. The main building had an old potbelly stove and a black-and-white television set, but the reception was bad because of the mountains.

'They set up the gear in one of the barns, and the boys would play all night and then sleep late. I was in charge of the cooking. Someone would hit off in the van and come back with crates of drink. There was a lot of drinking. But after a few weeks the boys started to get bored, stuck in the back of beyond, living on top of one another. The drink didn't help. There were rows. And he

124

was taking these pills that kept him awake so as he could work. The record, that's all he talked about.

'Some of the boys wanted to go back on the road and make money, but he was hell bent on finishing what he started. The pills and the drink were making him sick. He lost about a stone in weight, and there wasn't a pick on him in the first place.

'Then the stove packed in, and we ran out of firewood and started using the furniture for kindling. The boys lit out, one by one, back to Glasgow or London. So now it was just him and me and one or two stragglers. They'd go into the village every couple of days and make a few shillings busking or doing odd jobs. But the whole thing was starting to come apart. He got very strange.'

Her hair fell in her face. She tucked the stray strands behind her ears.

'Went into himself a-kinda. And one night he saw some programme on the telly and it gave him nightmares.'

'Nightmares?'

'Aye.'

'Like the ones I had?'

She stared at me. Her pupils were huge.

'His nerves went. He woke me up one night saying there was going to be a nuclear war that would wipe out most of the people on earth and those of us who were left would only be able to buy food or trade if we had a mark on our hands or foreheads. He said it was all foretold in the Bible, if you knew where to look.

'That was the last straw for the stragglers. They said they got into music to escape all that tripe. One night when he was out in the barn with the headphones on, I caught the last two lads loading gear into the van. They asked me to come with them, but I wouldn't.'

'Why not?'

'I just couldn't. I thought things would get better when the spring came. But they didn't. They only got worse. He tore up all these rubbish sacks and hung them over the windows. He said the RAF Harriers flying overhead were sent from a base to spy on us because we knew the truth. That the government was in the employment of the AntiChrist. Then he changed his mind and said the pilots of the planes were angels sent to watch over us. Then he decided the Third World War had already happened and the planes were remote controlled and they had government people on board, and they would just keep on refuelling over the earth until it was safe to land again. He warned me not to leave the farm or I couldn't come back cos I'd be poisoned from the radiation.'

'And you believed him?'

'I didn't know what to believe. When you're locked up with a sick person, John, you lose your grip on what's real. It's like wandering into a forest, and you stray so deep into the trees you lose your bearings. You don't know where to even start looking for a way back.

'Anyway, one night he was so crooked from the want of sleep he accidentally wiped a whole reel, weeks of work, and he came in and started throwing things around. He upended the table and a glass broke and nearly sliced my bare foot open. When I told him to calm down he raised his hand as if to strike me. That's when I decided to leave. If not for myself, for the baby.

'I was about ten weeks gone. I was afraid that when I started to show, he'd never let me leave. The state he was in, he would've thought I was going to give birth to Our Lord.'

She shivered a bit and pulled her cardigan tight around her shoulders.

'When I realised the condition I was in, I packed my bag and waited for the right time to make a move. He passed out one night after working about three days straight, so I took what money there was and sneaked out the door and ran down the lane. My heart was pounding. I was trying not to breathe too hard in case I took in poisonous gases. I sniffed the air for smoke and looked up at the sky to see if the world was covered with clouds of ash. I didn't meet a soul for ages and I was starting to wonder if the whole world was dead or not. Then I saw a man coming up the road, and half his face was covered in a big purple rash. I couldn't stop staring at it. I asked him was it from the fallout, and he said, 'No, love, I've had it my whole life, it's just a birthmark.'

'I stayed in the village that night and next day I hitched a lift south. I worked in a market in Edinburgh for a few weeks. I thought about him the whole time, wondering if he'd come after me. To tell you the god's honest truth, I was angry when he didn't. And I got vexed with myself and swore I'd never put my trust in another man again.'

Her face looked like it might crack into a hundred pieces.

'I saved my money until I had my fare home. When I arrived back, the door was shut in my face. Here I was showing up large after not sending word in months. I was afraid. I didn't know the first thing about childbearing. So I took a job as a maid in the hotel near the strand. That's where I met Phyllis Nagle. She was a quare old bird, but she was the only one who'd help me. I told her the fix I was in and she said she wouldn't see me stuck and found a caravan for me to rent. I worked until I was too far along to work any more. And when the time came, I had you. You were the savings of me.'

She stubbed out her cigarette and nodded, as if agreeing with herself.

'When you have a child, John, something changes in you. You're never free of worry. But you're never lonely neither.'

By now it was dark outside. The moon was huge and red. I drained my glass.

'Why are you telling me all this now?'

She pulled her cardigan tight.

'Because you're old enough. And because none of us know how much time is left.'

She poured us both another shot.

'When you get to my age, you have no more use for secrets.'

I reeled out into the night, Powers bottle in my hand, the old hymn burning in my mind and the road lurching like a funhouse floor. As soon as my mother had gone to bed I'd rung Jamey's house.

'What's up?' he said.

'Too wired to sleep. You around?'

He told me to meet him on the road into

the village. He sounded drunk. Which made two of us.

Now it was way past midnight, maybe going on for two o'clock. As I walked, I sang what I could remember of my mother's song to keep from getting spooked. The full moon burned inside its field of weirdly hued concentric rings, suspended like a huge balloon tethered to the chapel spire. The light it cast was bright enough for me to see Jamey coming from half a mile away. He was carrying a sports bag. We halted yards from each other, like duellists about to draw.

Jamey's clothes were rumpled and his hair was out of control.

'You look destroyed,' I said. 'Where've you been?'

The expression on his face was close to sheepish.

'I was trying to keep up with Gunter.'

Being able to hold his drink was a point of honour with Jamey. He rubbed his hollow cheeks and shook his head.

'I heard some stuff, man,' he said. 'Scary. Think I'm out of my depth with those boys.'

'What kind of stuff?'

'You'd be better off not knowing.'

I took a slug of whiskey and offered Jamey some.

'Jesus,' he said. 'Where'd you get that?'

'My mother.'

'Your mother is a great woman.'

He took a mouthful, raised the bottle in a toast and handed it back, then unzipped the sports bag and pulled out a battered-looking camcorder.

'Found this in the Superstores.' He fiddled with the lens cap. 'Secondhand, but it works.' He put the camera to his eye, panning over the fields. It felt like we were the first colonisers of some remote, lonely planet.

'Let's walk,' he said. 'I want to shoot some stuff for my film.'

Now he was a filmmaker.

'It'll be a whatchamacallit,' he said. 'A bio-pic. You can play Verlaine. I'll be Rimbaud. We'll call it *Merde à Dieu*.'

We wandered the outskirts of Kilcody for ages, Jamey filming anything he found interesting, which was everything, and when our feet got sore we stopped for a smoke, passing the whiskey back and forth until it was gone. The moonlight was so strong it felt like a tractor beam that might suck us right up off the earth. I stepped into the gripe to fling the empty bottle over a ditch and in the process got something on my runners. I stood stork-like on the road and hopped a bit. My laces were stained with grass juice. A tapioca-like substance was smeared all over the patterned rubber soles.

'Cow shit?' Jamey said.

'Frogspawn.'

I scraped it off on the grass, struggling to keep my balance. I'd never been so drunk. We shambled towards the village.

'What now?' I said when we reached the square.

'We could go back to my place,' Jamey said. 'Free house.'

I pointed towards the chapel.

'Or we could shoot some interiors.' The words felt strange in my mouth. I had to concentrate to make them come out the right shape. 'You can't have a film called *Merde à Dieu* without any Jesus action in it.'

I began to cross the square. Jamey trotted after me.

'Hang on,' he called out. I ignored him and grabbed the wrought iron bars of the chapel gates and pulled myself up and over. He peered through the bars as I clapped flecks of rusty paint from my hands.

'How we gonna get inside?' he said.

'We'll jimmy the lock or something.' It suddenly seemed important. 'Trust me.'

The way Jamey was staring, I could see my face reflected in his irises, just as his must have been reflected in mine, mirrored eyes replicating images of each other off into for ever.

Jesus don't show me your nightmare, I'll show you mine.

The chapel's mouth opens and the darkness sucks me in. My bare feet leave heat imprints on the cold flagstones. The faintest sounds are amplified and echo in the vaulted roof. Stone saints turn their heads, moonlight streams through the stained-glass windows.

This dark crypt is infested with musty shadows and trapped whispers. Hairs grow from the sweating walls, and the holy water font bubbles over, beads of mercury slithering across the floor. I approach the altar, footfall over footfall, echo upon echo. The Stations of the Cross unfold on either side like fourteen frames of a strange snuff film.

I pause at the altar railings and lift my head.

Under the INRI, Christ slumps from the cross, head turned away as if trying to avoid the kiss of a stalker-fan. The emaciated body of a supermodel, luminous in the stained-glass light.

Or lack of it.

The silence makes me gag.

Put your hand against my chest, feel the smell fill my lungs like flu. It's everywhere. This incense sleeps against the church rafters like gas. You can taste the rising damp, smell the must, feel the chill, see the mist, hear the trickle-down drip-drip-drip. Something worse than incense fills my nose and mouth and I breathe it in and the chapel hisses with gas-leak whispers. The stink grows thick, burns my throat.

(Lord I am not worthy to receive you.)

Christ's eyes glow red and bore through me.

(Father, forgive me.)

Merde à Dieu

(Where are you?)

Eloi, eloi sabacthani.

(Cá? Cá?)

Have I offended thee?

A finger against his lips.

Shhh.

See no, hear no, speak no evil.

(Bless me father for I have sinned. It's been a lifetime since my last confession.)

And now the chapel bell sounds, the sacred heart burns, God is on his throne and the world is doomed. Angels hold the four winds back. The tabernacle has been forced. The apocalypse is out. The seventh seal is open, and for half an hour all heaven is in silence.

The smell rises up, curdling the water in my mouth, the bland wafer taste on my tongue. And my prints are all over the place, a genetic stain, a confession that can't be retracted.

Pain spears my stomach. Bile rises up my neck. Clothing falls away in tattered scraps and I am naked.

Noise erupts.

The roof caves in.

Stars go out.

Rain pours down and puddles in the hollows of the broken floor, rises, spreads, the floor bows under the water's weight. It gets cold so fast, the water freezes.

Under the ice, faces.

My face.

I turn to run.

My feet melt the ice; tongues lick my feet.

The ice cracks, the floor gives way and I fall into a pit of mouths.

And fall and keep on falling through the mouths, through the tongues.

I hit the floor.

The floor gives way.

I fall some more.

I hit the bottom, a broken puppet in an open coffin.

The lid slams shut and I'm trapped in a lead-lined box, blind, deaf and dumb, a limbless thing whose mind whirls in circles, devouring its own reason. Worms gnaw through the wood, mute heads burrowing. They can't hear, but their wormskin feels me breathing.

I breathe the smell.

Is this the blood of the lamb on my tongue? Or the devil's excrement on my hands?

6

The telephone's ringing shrilled through the house and corkscrewed into my sleep. I tried to open my eyes but they were all gummed up. I blinked until the blur cleared. Cruel sunlight made me squint.

'Ma?'

No answer.

I pulled on my jeans and hurried downstairs, lifted the receiver from its cradle.

'Hello.'

My voice was raspy from smoke and drink. I'd moved too suddenly: my stomach growled.

Jamey's voice grated through the receiver: 'What in the hell got into you?'

He sounded angry. Not just angry. Scared.

'What — '

Dry mouth. My tongue was swollen. It hurt to swallow.

'You went *berserk*,' he said. 'In the church. What's wrong with you, man?'

His voice was so loud I had to hold the phone away from my ear for a second. I felt dizzy.

'Is this a joke?'

'No, it's not a joke. We fucked up. Badly.'

Everything was way too bright.

'Jamey, tell me what happened. I think I blacked out.'

'Oh for god's sake.'

He sighed. It came out as static.

'Look, you flipped.'

He spoke slowly, as though explaining something to a child.

'You started breaking stuff . . . '

Fragments of dream and memory began to detach themselves from the murk and float to the surface, horrible as jumbled bits of bodies.

' . . . I had to drag you out of there. You took off like a loon.'

I put my head against the wall, a horrible hot-cold sweat breaking from my pores. I breathed in and out, trying to expel all the hot, sickly air from my stomach. Far away, Jamey's voice squawked and crackled but I couldn't make out the words.

There was a knock on the door.

'I feel sick,' I mumbled. 'I have to go.'

The phone fell off the cradle and dangled from its cord. Another knock. The walls seemed to tilt as I felt my way to the door. Through frosted glass, the silhouette of a man. I twisted the latch. Guard Canavan stood before me on the step. Older than I remembered, starting to grey.

'John Devine?' he said.

'Yes.'

The squad car was parked at our gate. He looked me up and down.

'Get dressed.'

'Where we going?'

His eyes were hard as stones.

'The barracks.'

There were two of them, Guard Canavan and a plainclothes man. They questioned me for ages, but all I could focus on was a bluebottle circling the light bulb, buzzing like a tiny chainsaw. No windows in the room, just a table and a couple of hard chairs. On the floor was a VCR player rigged up to a portable television set. Wires everywhere. It was unbearably humid; the place stank of white-scared sweat.

The plainclothes man sat on the table, a notepad flipped open. Every question I answered — who am I, where do I live, where was I last night — he wrote something. Every question I asked, he ignored. The bluebottle buzzed. The room stank. Guard Canavan stood at my shoulder; I had to twist in my chair to see his face.

'We want to show you something,' the plainclothes man said, and pressed a button on the VCR. Canavan moved to the wall and flicked off the light switch. The bluebottle went quiet. The television screen flickered, casting chiaroscuro shadows across the floor, the silence shattered by a blast of white noise.

A stream of blurry images filled the screen. Camcorder capture, jerky and hand-held. A queasy feeling in the pit of my stomach, a stone hitting water, sinking down into my bowels. My shoulders knotted as the lens sharpened and the images came into focus. Close up: a page ripped from a notebook, biro scrawled in a ragged hand.

Merde à Dieu.

The title card.

'Recognise the writing?' Canavan said.

The camera panned to the tabernacle, zoomed into Jesus on the cross, and then a jarring cut to a perfect circle of white. The Eucharist. The camera pulled back. Communion wafers were strewn about the carpeted floor of the altar. A face filled the screen, curtained by hair. The plainclothes man paused the tape. It was my face, frozen under glass. Superimposed upon it, my reflection, staring from across the room. Canavan spoke into my ear, so close I could smell smoke and mouthwash.

'Who was holding the camera?'

I looked at the floor. My runners were still

stained with grass juice.

'I don't know.'

'You know. And unless you tell me, I'm going to charge you right this minute.'

'With what?'

'You want me to draw you a picture?'

'No, I just want to know what you're accusing me of.'

Canavan nodded.

'All right. The front door of the chapel was forced. One of the statues was toppled and smashed in bits. The tabernacle was driven in with one of those big brass candle-holders. There was Holy Communion thrown around everywhere. The chalice is still missing. And there was excrement on the altar. Faeces. Somebody used the place for a toilet, John.'

He was lying about the last part. Had to be.

'What kind of cur do you think would do that?' he said.

The plainclothes man stood and stretched.

'We should show him the rest,' he said. 'Maybe that'll jog his memory.'

They played the tape. I saw the shape of my body in the murk, facing the cross, a shadow speared by diagonal shafts of moonlight streaming through the stained glass, and just for a second I saw my whole shape change, become something else, something bestial, a goat if a goat could stand on its hind legs, something with long twisted nails and hair down its back and hoofs for feet and it *howled*, the sound so loud it overloaded the camcorder's microphone and then the camera whipped away and all you could see was blackness, all you could hear was my voice, the sound torn from my throat, inchoate, violently distorted.

My fingers clawed at my jeans. I remembered the speech Canavan gave to our class when I was small, a ridiculous speech about what happened to bad boys and girls who went to hell, and it struck me that he was a religious man, and that chilled my heart. A small voice inside me started babbling an act of contrition, but all it could remember was the first line and the rest came out garbled.

I looked from Canavan to the plainclothes man, but they seemed not to have seen what I'd seen on the tape. Stuff came up my neck; I cupped a hand to my mouth. Canavan lunged for my arm and pulled me out of the room and down a hall and into another room with a toilet and a washbasin. I hung my head over the toilet bowl but nothing came up, so I stuck my fingers down my throat and dry-heaved until my stomach hurt. Spat. Rinsed my mouth with water from the tap.

Looked in the mirror. My eyes were like burn holes in a sheet.

Canavan leaned against the door, arms folded.

'What were you on?'

'Huh?'

'You were on something. What was it?'

'I wasn't on anything.'

'That's not what it looked like.'

'Swear to god.'

'We can do tests. It'll still be in your bloodstream.'

'Do all the tests you want.'

'Someone put you up to this, didn't they? Whoever was holding the camera. And I've a pretty good idea who it was.'

He cleared his throat.

'In fact, we've already interviewed him. He said he saw you going into the church that night.'

'You're lying. He wouldn't.'

'So you know who I'm talking about?'

Shit.

'C'mon, John. Don't suffer that lad any favours. He wouldn't do the same for you. All you have to do is tell me his name.'

I wiped my mouth with the back of my hand.

'No can do.'

'Well, son, if you don't, I'm going to charge you. It'll make the papers. You're a minor, so they mightn't be able to print the details, but it's a small village. Everyone will know. You'll have that on your head for as long as you live in Kilcody.'

He reached for the door.

'I should call your mother. She'll want to contact her solicitor. That'll put a hole in her pocket.' He shook his head. 'She'll be disappointed. She taught you better.'

'Hang on,' I said.

He paused, one hand on the door handle. I swallowed sour spit.

'If I tell you, what happens?'

'It all depends.'

'On what?'

'On what you tell me.'

'What if I give you a name?'

'Then I'll see what I can do.'

I wiped my palms on my shirt.

'And my mother doesn't have to know?'

'You co-operate and I'll think about it. Your mother doesn't need this on her head.'

I closed my eyes. I imagined Canavan calling my mother. The look on her face as she held the phone to her ear. A court summons arriving in the post. My mother withdrawing money from her savings account and calling a solicitor.

I felt sick in my heart.

I could've told him anything. I could've

lied through my teeth. Or I could've told him what he wanted to know. Everything.

It's not what goes in your mouth.

'Jamey Corboy.'

It's what comes out.

In the sluggish, humid weeks that followed, the village seemed unreal, a heat mirage. People moved in slow motion through the market square. Buildings slumped into their foundations as though melted by the heat, and the shadows they cast were crooked and long.

The chapel cast the longest shadow of all.

I remembered what Father Quinn told us when we were preparing for our Confirmation, that hell isn't necessarily a place full of devils and demons and people burning in everlasting lakes of fire, hell can simply mean an absence of God.

Religious objects appeared everywhere. The sacred-heart lamp in the kitchen. The crucified Christ shackled to the rosary beads my mother kept on her bedside locker. The plastic Madonna filled with holy water that Mrs Nagle brought us back from Lourdes one year, its sad mother's eyes downcast and crestfallen.

I sat on the monument most afternoons and watched the swimmers set off for the Soldier's Hole, rowdy, lanky youths with towels and togs tucked under their arms. I envied how easy in their skin they seemed, how careless and sure of themselves, as though they'd never known what it meant to feel separate, trapped under the magnified sun like an ugly insect under glass. Wretched and unclean.

The nights were the worst. The air was suffocating and clammy and close. Endlessly, obsessively, I replayed the memory of that morning in the barracks when I spilled my guts about the break-in at the chapel, about Jamey and Gunter stealing drink and cigarettes from The Ginnet. The darkness swirled with stories I'd read about sleepwalkers who commited murder, or drunks who blacked out and perpetrated abominable acts and woke up none the wiser except for the stains on their hands. I lay in bed, exhausted and sticky with sweat, the sheets twisted into knots.

One morning I came downstairs to find my mother sat at the kitchen table, the *Ballo Sentinel* spread out before her.

'You got a letter in the post,' she said, indicating the mess of brochures and bills and junk mail that had accumulated in the middle of the table. I found the letter and tore open the envelope, and my stomach rolled over when I recognised Jamey's spidery handwriting, the letters crammed together like lifeboat passengers. I took it out onto the front step where I could read it in privacy.

15 Fairview Crescent
Ballo Town

Well, John,

A lot of effluent has passed under the overhang since last we spoke. As you can see from the address, this letter comes to you from the extraordinarily unremarkable hamlet of Ballo town. Yes, it came to pass that Maurice put the house up for sale and we moved back here. They said it was to be nearer me when I have to go, so they can visit more often, but I think it's cos they couldn't bear to show their faces in Kilcody any more.

By now you'll have heard that they gave me a year on remand in Balinbagin Boys' Home. Dee keeps asking why I did it, but I can hardly enlighten her, can I? You'd be better qualified to answer that one. You got away jammy, my friend, but I don't begrudge you a bit of it. Let's just blame it on old Rimbaud, shall we? Maybe we took him a bit too literally.

I've been thinking about what happened but I can't say too much for obvious reasons. Never put anything incriminating in writing. Or on tape.

I won't forget that little lesson.

I can't remember much about the trial, except our solicitor wanted it done and dusted, fast. There was a lot of muttering and legal jargon and barrister language and the judge asked me how I pleaded and I said, 'Guilty, your honour,' just like they told me. It's a strange thing to say those words in a court of law. I didn't understand what was going on most of the time, at least not until the judge handed down my sentence. I understood that well enough.

The solicitor said I'd probably only serve six months tops. I'm not worried, to be honest. These places are not what they used to be. Tell you the truth, I'm more concerned about Gunter. Apparently he thinks I shopped him over the Ginnet job and various other business enterprises it'd be unwise to mention in writing. I never said a word. The big lug can't blame me if there's a stoolie in his camp.

The sooner I start serving my sentence the better. Incarceration is probably the safest thing for me!

Anyway, gotta go.

People to see, stuff to do.

Or not.

Later,

Jamey

I folded the letter and shoved it into my pocket. When I went back into the kitchen my mother was squinting at the newspaper. The optician had prescribed reading glasses but she refused to wear them, said they made her look like a librarian. Her face was set in a scowl.

'Good lord,' she said. 'Did you know anything about this?'

'About what?'

She tapped the front page of the paper and passed it to me. It was the second item, after a big piece about the introduction of parking discs. I scanned the story and did my best to approximate an expression of horror.

Local Youth Convicted of Chapel Desecration

... the chapel was so seriously *desecrated* — consecrated hosts were removed, and the altar was defecated upon — that a rededication ceremony was held before Mass could be celebrated there again. Police have not ruled out rumours of local youths involved in *bizarre Satanic cult rituals* . . .

'Jesus,' I said.
'Language, John.'
'Sorry.'
I could feel her eyes on me as I read it more closely.
'It says he admitted it,' she said, her face inscrutable. I put the paper down and went to the sink and got a glass of water. She stood with her back against the table, arms folded.
'Did Jamey ever mention this to you?'
'This is the first I heard of it.'
Her mouth curled.
'I find that hard to believe.'
Something made me think of those true crime stories where they know the murderer is guilty if he's able to fall asleep in the interrogation room.
'Someone must have put him up to it,' I said.
'I wonder.' My mother unfolded her arms and shook her head. 'He seemed like such a nice chap. But I can tell you right now, that's the last you'll see of him, in or out of Balinbagin. If any son of mine got up to that kind of carry-on, no matter how hardy he

was, I'd box the two ears off of him. And then I'd let the Guards deal with it.'

'You'd do right,' I said.

She harrumphed and washed out her mug and went into the bathroom to get washed.

I sat at the table and went through the rest of the paper. My eye caught on one of the headlines dominating the features pages.

Missing Asylum Seeker Feared Victim of Human Trafficking Ring

by Jason Davin, Staff Reporter

Fears are on the rise that Jude Udechukwu, the 20-year-old Nigerian asylum-seeker who disappeared from Kilcody recently, could have been the target of gangs using the threat of black magic in order to coerce innocent victims into slavery.

Last week the *Sentinel* office received a telephone call from a man alleging himself to be friends with the Nigerian. He wished to be identified only by the name Okenawe. He said he was flatmates with Mr Udechukwu and a number of other illegal immigrants earlier this year in West London.

According to the caller, Mr Udechukwu

said in January he was kidnapped by several men in the city of Lagos in Nigeria one evening and driven to a derelict house on the outskirts of the city. He was gagged and bound to a chair and held captive for several hours. For the duration of his ordeal, his face was smeared with blood and he was forced to eat animal parts. He was eventually set free and instructed to return with a large sum of money within 24 hours. If he failed, he was told he would be *decapitated* and his family cursed.

In what was later revealed to have been part of the scam, Mr Udechukwu was contacted by a man who offered him a chance of escape, using forged documentation and a plane ticket. He flew to London via Milan, where he was given a mobile phone and told to await further instructions. It was there he met Mr Okenawe.

Over a period of some months, both men were involved in various benefit-fraud rackets, in which they were forced to make a monthly repayment, plus interest, to a local contact, for 'expenses' (airline fare, fake passport, accommodation). They shared a room with a dozen other men and women, some of them teenagers. Most of the girls were involved in *prostitution* or employed as poorly paid servants. If they did not maintain their payments, they were warned, their bosses would use supernatural powers to find their families and kill them.

According Mr Okenawe, as the weeks went on Mr Udechukwu grew more fraught of ever clearing his debt and spoke of fleeing London. He said the plan was to hitch-hike to Swansea and take a ferry to Ireland. After he disappeared, Mr Okenawe assumed that was what had happened. When an Irish friend showed him this newspaper's report of Mr Udechukwu's disappearance some weeks back, he contacted the *Sentinel* office. Mr Okenawe fears that Mr Udechukwu may have been tracked down and even killed by members of the gang who were *blackmailing* him.

Incidents of 'muti' or 'obeah' ritual killings, while still rare in the West, have been on the rise recently. Some years ago the headless body of a man was found floating in the Liffey, and last year in the Midlands, a disembodied *torso* was found in a suitcase. The Zulu word 'muti' is shorthand for any medicine practised by sangomas, or traditional South African healers. 'Obeah' is a form of witchcraft. It involves the human sacrifice of a pre-pubescent.

The practice of black-magic medicine has given rise to a thriving trade in recent times. Several years ago the South African government set up an inquiry into witchcraft and ritual murders after a spate of kidnappings and deaths in Soweto. Investigations revealed that the harvesting of *brains* and *reproductive organs* of one person could fetch thousands of pounds. The organs of Caucasian men were deemed even more valuable, because of their business prowess. Reports revealed that body parts removed from live victims were considered more valuable because the screams of the victims made them potent. The vast majority of traditional healers will have nothing to do with the trade, but anyone with enough money can buy remedies made from human body parts.

When contacted by the *Sentinel*, a local Garda spokesman said they are taking Mr Okenawe's claims seriously. They are currently considering a full investigation.

I folded the paper, strangely comforted.

Days crawled by on their bellies. Books were a poor substitute for Jamey's company. I was bored out of my mind, and it didn't take long for my mother to become browned off with my presence.

'John,' she said, 'you can't mope around the house all summer. We may find you a job.'

'What kind of job?'

'Nicky Gibbons is hiring pickers.'

She'd obviously thought this one out in advance. One phone call and I was hired.

We all gathered at the pick-up spot on the crossroads at half six on the dot. Nicky's Renault 4 pulled up and a bunch of us crammed in, mostly kids my age or younger, clutching buckets and tubs, clothes caked with dried muck. Nicky dropped us off at the gate and drove off to collect the next crew. We dragged ourselves through the yard and assembled on the headland. The air still had traces of early morning chill. I cast my eyes across the field, rows and rows of dew-drenched strawberry plants stretching off into the next county.

We got to work, feet planted on either side of the drills, fingers groping through the leaves. The sleeves of my jumper were soon drenched and my wrists itched and the sickly sweet fruit juice stung the hangnails on my fingers. All morning an unnatural quiet hung over everything, disturbed only by the rustling of plants. Sometimes I heard strains of music drifting queerly from the depths of the mist and I stared off at the surrounding landscape, feeling like a convict on a prison road crew, contemplating the freedom beyond the ditches.

Sometimes I wondered what it would be like to set off across those fields and disappear into the whispering woods, just vanish into the will-o'-the-wisp, become a ghost drifting through narrow laneways, to walk until it felt like I no longer existed, like I had already died, hit by lightning or one of those big articulated trucks bound for Ballo harbour, so suddenly that my soul could not escape my mouth and got trapped in some purgatorial realm of in-between things, doomed to following my shadow, my shadow following me, and sometimes two shadows walking in tandem, another me and another Jamey.

I tried to shake off the mood and get back to work.

When my bucket was full I lugged it to the top of the drill and dumped its contents into a blue plastic tray, and when that was full — three buckets did the job — I slotted a second tray on top. My backside was soggy from squatting in mashed fruit. My back ached and I had to keep changing posture to get any relief.

Pickers moved steadily down the drills, grubs working on a carcass. The plants dried out as the sun crawled up the sky's curvature. The first break was at eleven. Nicky's wife Greta brought the teapot and we all lined up with our mugs. I sat on my coat and ate my ploughman sandwiches and listened to the other pickers discuss the weather, and if it would hold, and if it rained what kind of rain would it be, because a shower would mean we'd wait in the haggart and drink tea until it passed and then get back to work, but anything heavier meant we'd be rained off altogether and have to come back another day. Nicky was always loath to let that happen; he had a harvest to bring in. No matter how dismal the downpour he'd stand in the doorway of the haggart and looking off into the sky say, 'I think it's clearing up, lads,' and a chorus of voices would assure him that no, he was seeing things, it was down for the day.

The other pickers were a motley lot. The Flynn twins were only nine or ten but could pick more buckets per day than I could manage in a week. I made a point of stacking my trays as far away from them as possible in order to minimise the humiliation. And there was Larry Mythen, a red-headed giant, six foot plus in his socks. They said he got violent when he was jarred and that he'd done time in gaol. I looked at his open face and gentle eyes and couldn't picture it. Then there was Carol Cassidy, tall and coltish, with sparkling eyes and long brown hair, skin-tight jeans tucked into her wellingtons. I was village-idiot smitten, but she only lasted a week before she found better things to do with her summer. And then there was Trigger Quigly, a squat little sparkplug of a man who sprayed spittle when he spoke. He seemed harmless enough, but all the women gave him a wide berth and said he was a dirty bugger.

After I'd eaten my sandwiches at break I swapped my bourbon creams for two cigarettes from a chap with a harelip and smoked them an inch at a time, carefully dousing the tips with spit and placing the butts in my shirt pocket.

The pickers filed back into the drills. Towards the last part of the day my mind wandered and I got careless, filling my bucket with hard white berries that hadn't ripened yet and soft mushy ones that came apart in balls of must.

Around five o'clock Nicky appeared on the headland to tally up the numbers in a ledger. He went through my trays plucking out the

158

bad berries and asked me to take a bit more care in the quality-control department. We stacked the trays in the trailer for delivery to the fruit factory. It was hard work.

When I got home in the evenings I was fit for nothing but dinner and bed. My hands were permanently stained with grime and juice. I slept deep and dreamless and when the alarm went off I put my filthy clothes back on and packed my lunch and waited at the gate. Every morning I prayed for a rain-off. Two more weeks passed, and then the drills would yield only shrivelled kernels. Nicky Gibbons dropped round to the house with my cheque and told me it had been a pleasure and if I was interested he'd hired a bus to take us to the amusements at Ballo harbour for a day out and would I come. I told him that sounded like fun and he could count me in.

The morning the bus was due to take us to Ballo, another letter arrived for me. I stuffed it in my jacket and hurried to the crossroads. The regulars were barely recognisable in their clean T-shirts and pressed pants, faces scrubbed and hair washed. Their excitement was infectious. We boarded the bus, the younger kids already getting stuck into their sweets and bags of crisps, the rowdy ones horsing around in the back seats. As the bus pulled out, I opened Jamey's letter and began to read.

15 Fairview Crescent
Ballo Town

John,

I had this dream, this really trippy dream where I was in hell, then I woke up and I was in hell, dreaming. Anyway, the dream started with me in court. The judge passed sentence and the stenographer typed and the cops clapped me in irons and took me down into a sort of an ante-room and stripped me, and the gaoler came, a no-faced man with yellow fangs, and he pulled on a rubber glove, made a fist, ordered me to touch the floor and said, 'Spread 'em like jam, son.' And when he was finished having his evil way with my innards the guards brought me to the showers, blasted me with hoses and powdered me with delousing powder and disinfectant and made me carry my kit around and around until we paused at a kind of vestibule and the gaoler said, 'Read it and weep, son.'

I read it — *Abandon hope ye who enter here* — and we kept walking until we came to a door.

'This is the hellovator,' said the gaoler. A computerised voice droned, *Going down.* The lift lurched and I watched the light above the door, counting off the levels, one to nine. There were yellow Post-Its stuck to each number, and the door opened at each floor.

1 — *the virtuous pagans and unbaptised children*
We saw feral brats rummaging in rubbish.

2 — *the carnal*
Leprous beggars in drag wriggling through the gutters, mewling for alms.

3 — *the gluttonous*
Jabba The Hut munching a moneyburger.

4 — *the hoarders and the wasters*
An amputee stuffed in a box in someone's basement, a stick of yellow chalk gripped between its teeth, scrawling *kill me* on the wood.

5 — *the wrathful and the sullen*
A television crew moving through empty rape rooms.

6 — *the heretics*

A pig walking upright through a shopping mall, the horrified shoppers recoiling.

And then, when we got to Level 7 — *the bestial and the violent; the murderers and mongers of war; the suicides and sodomites, the blasphemers, perverts and usurers* — the gaoler said, 'This is your floor. They're gonna love you here.'

We stepped into a gleaming corridor and the air went shrill with whistles. Beady eyes glared from the cells. In one cubicle a young fellow was taking blasts from an inhaler and trying to staunch bleeding from his you-know-where with wet toilet paper.

'My first Penitentiary period,' said the kid.

We moved on. A snivelling little gom came along pushing a laundry cart full of yarns. He stopped, looked left and right, and said, 'Story?'

'What price?' the gaoler asked.

'Half notten, boss,' the gom answered, so the gaoler put a coin in a slot in the gom's forehead, and the gom began to recite by rote.

'This is about a fat boy called Roy Caulfield,' he said, 'who on his first day inside, caught the eye of Paws O'Rourke. Paws took a fancy to this lovely little cutlet, but Roy made the mistake of putting up a fight, kicking and squealing and calling Paws dirty names. So Paws, he says, 'If you're going to talk like a potty-mouth, we'll use you for one.' And they dragged the lad to the infirmary, strapped him into the dentist's chair, pulled every tooth from his head and fitted his jaws with a clamp. And for three days and three nights every man and jack on level seven mounted that dentist's chair and used the chap's gummy gob for a scumbag.'

The gom winked and gimped off with his cart.

The gaoler spat on his cigarette, and it hissed.

'Come on,' he said. 'You should meet the boss before I swipe you in.'

Wilting with the heat, we got back in the lift.

Going down.

Level 8 — *the fraudulent and malicious, panderers and seducers, flatterers, simoniacs, fortune-tellers and diviners, hypocrites, thieves, evil counsellors, falsifiers: alchemists, counterfeiters and false witnesses*
A politburo meeting.

Going down.

Level 9 — Mongers of compound fraud, the treacherous to kinsmen and to country, and to their guests and hosts and masters The belly of hell.

Said the gaoler, 'Warden's been expecting.'
But I knew already, by the smell: Brother Bubba Ze Bel.
Bubba stood, arms open wide, his pits wafting, big fat smiley head on him.

'Welcome, son,' he said, rubbing the chalk from his hands. We shook. He tickled my palm with his pinky and gave me a playful slap across the cheek.

This is the part where I wake for real, in a slick of sweat. I have this dream a lot, John.

What do you think it means? More to the point, why have you forsaken me?

Your friend,
Jamey

All day I wandered aimlessly from Ferris wheel to ghost train to paddle boats. Speakers blared horrendously distorted rinky-dink music, generators belched fumes and everything smelled of smoke and diesel. I drifted through the arcade, flinching at the pandemonium, and pumped coppers into one-armed bandits and shot a few games of pool with people I didn't know. The dodgems banged crazily into each other and the waltzers lurched, and for a moment I thought I saw Mrs Nagle's face, contorted with g-force, eyes wide and mouth opened and shrieking like a banshee, but when I looked again she was gone.

People milled along the promenade. Rows of stalls and tables laden with cheap jewellery, gimcrack stuff, necklaces and rings and charms and amulets and stones. Caravans with signs in the windows advertising Tarot and palm and crystal-ball readings. I counted my money and went up the steps to one of the caravans and knocked on the open door. A woman in a baggy jumper and a pair of sweatpants was watching a portable television blaring some sort of game show. She turned the sound down and waved a hand at an armchair beside a flimsy table.

'Fiver for your palm, tenner for the cards,' she said.

I gave her a tenner. She donned a pair of glasses and took my hand and pulled my fingers apart and peered at the lines. Her head jerked up. She stared at my face.

'Out,' she said.

'What?'

'Out.' She pushed the tenner across the table. 'And take your money with you.'

I stood and backed out the doorway and stumbled down the steps and into the night. The door slammed and the blinds came down. The funfair whirled around me. Lights seemed to liquefy into luminous streaks as I blundered down the promenade under the glimmering big wheel. Figures loomed out of darkness and vanished, skeletons prancing through a Mardi Gras carnival. Young men chatted and flirted with sassy-faced girls with ponytails and bangle-sized ear-rings as they locked safety bars across the seats on the Skyrider. A black goatee-bearded man in a bright yellow shirt and snazzy shoes did card tricks for a small crowd, gaudy rings gleaming on his quick fingers.

Then I saw Miss Ross, the replacement English teacher, all dolled up in mascara and eye shadow, her hair teased out, and she was walking arm in arm with a boy barely older than me, and they were laughing, faces aglow. They stopped and kissed. The boyfriend felt the cheeks of Miss Ross's bottom through her mini-skirt and I watched, gobsmacked, couldn't look away until they were swept downstream by the crowd's current.

I wandered through the commotion. A young cleanshaven man was handing out pamphlets, trying to keep his cool as he was pestered and harangued by crop-haired little toughies. He handed me one of the leaflets and moved on. The cover said: *ARE THESE THE LAST DAYS?* The pages were filled with admonitions about men becoming lovers of money and pleasure, children disobeying parents, nations rising up against each other, earthquakes, food shortages, pestilences. The centre spread showed images of juvenile delinquents packing Uzis. Bible quotes. Global climate changes and markets crashing. This stuff was called the Good News. I put the pamphlet in my pocket beside Jamey's letter and hurried back to the car park.

The blue-tinted lights were on in the coach, and its engine was running. I climbed on board and took a seat at the back, away from the wired, white-faced children and jarred adults staggering in the aisle. Somebody had thrown up; you could smell it. As the bus revved and shuddered and pulled off, I put my head against the window and gazed into the gloom and wished I were far away.

I must have dozed off, lulled by the vibration of the engine, because when I opened my eyes Nicky Gibbons was stood in the aisle calling my name.

'John,' he said, 'we'll let you off at the crossroads.'

The coach hissed to a stop. Nicky shook my hand.

'See you next year,' he said.

I got off the bus and stood on the roadside and looked up at the sky and thought for a second I saw Jamey's face, wan and haunted, mapped in the pitted topography of that summer moon.

A newsflash, a tickertape snake sidewinding across the bottom of the screen. The doe-eyed anchor, eyebrows plucked into pencilled arches, make-up flawless, abandons the autocue for a printout thrust on her desk.

'We interrupt our scheduled news programming to bring you this bulletin.'

Her voice wavers. Tears bubble over kohl rims.

'The final seal has been opened. This is not a hoax. We go live now to London.'

Cut to satellite phone feed rendered cubist by signal crack-up.

'I'm sorry, but we seem to be encountering some technical difficulties. We now join our correspondent in Berlin.'

Cut to baby-faced boys packing Kalashnikovs, posted outside public buildings.

Cut to Sydney, digicam footage of riots and looters shot on sight.

'More updates as they happen . . . '

Hong Kong: office blocks with shutters pulled down, blue neon signs dying, curfews, queues for food, mobbed hospital wards.

'24-hour rolling news, the world as it

169

happens, in your home . . . '

Los Angeles: turnpikes jammed with rusting cars, fiftymile gridlock in every direction. Black helicopters swarm the skies like flies.

Cut to: Dead air at primetime.

A death's-head test card.

Cut.

The power goes out, the images shrink into a small white dot.

I get to my feet and walk out of the house and climb into a car. The car drives itself, merging with a torrent of tail-backed traffic, fleets of vehicles bound for the beach, converging on the seaside car park jammed with chip vans. Droves of people mill towards the waterline; some of them clutch bottles of iodine pills like religious icons, some drink from flagons, some smoke dope, anything to numb the panicky-euphoric feeling of this is happening.

Two blokes wearing billabong hats carry a cross improvised from railroad girders to the shore and lay it flat on the sand. A third man in a too-tight suit lies across it, his comb-over unwinding like a turban in the sea wind. They nail him through the wrists and ankles and raise it up. He hangs like a side of beef, bawling his head off, but they haven't planted the cross deep enough and it tilts slowly forward and hits the wet sand, the sounds of his torment muffled, mouth clogged up with silt.

Everyone has that sweaty and elated look marathon runners get at the twenty-mile mark. Thousands of flushed faces face the sea, gasping spectators at a fireworks display. Breakers lash the sand, foaming beasts bolt the flaming city and here it comes, rearing across the sound like a mile-high wall of lava, like Krakatoa exploding, and you can feel the heat, the air so thick with flying ash and chemicals and death you can barely breathe. We can't tear our eyes away.

We were never warned that it would look so beautiful.

7

The Patron was a big open-air concelebrated Mass that brought crowds from all over the parish every August. We'd been cleaning my grandparents' grave for hours, toiling under the stare of the great stone archangel that surveyed the buried dead from its vantage point on the raised plinth.

My mother doused the headstone using a squirt bottle filled with a solution of water and washing-up liquid. Elbows and foreams pumping, sweat shining on her brow, she scrubbed and scoured the headstone with a Brillo pad, pausing every so often to catch her breath. The summer heat had taken its toll. She placed her hands on her hips and scrutinised my face.

'What's the matter, John?' She groaned as she straightened her back. 'You're very quiet.'

I shrugged and said, 'Nothing.'

She wrenched up a bunch of what looked like clover, bits of dirt dropping from the roots.

'C'mon,' she said. 'Don't make me get the pliers out.'

I looked blearily at the sun and said, 'I had a weird dream last night.'

She dumped the weeds in a pile.

'You and your dreams. What was it about?'

'The world was ending.'

She picked up a bit of an old dishrag and wiped her hands, took out her cigarettes and lit one.

'Tell me more. Maybe I can make sense of it.'

'It doesn't matter. It was stupid.'

'Tell me anyway. Just for pig iron.'

I described what I could remember of the dream. She listened and nodded, smoke seeping out her nostrils.

'People have been seeing the end of time since time began,' she said. 'After Our Lord was crucified and ascended to heaven, the apostles thought the world was about to end. When that didn't happen, they all started writing things down. If not for the end of the world never happening, there'd be no gospels. Same with the first millennium.'

I waited for her to continue, but she didn't.

'What happened at the first millennium?' I said.

'Nothing. They thought the world would end in the year one thousand, and when it didn't, they moved the date to the anniversary of the crucifixion.'

She tapped ash onto the pile of weeds at her feet.

'By the Middle Ages, there were so many lunatics running around England predicting the end of the world, they made talking about the Second Coming a criminal offence. That's why so many of 'em hit off to America.'

She gazed at the inscription on the marble stone, obsidian flecked with white. People picked their way through the graves dressed in their best clothes, careful not to twist their ankles on sods of muck. In a couple of hours the cemetery would be thronged, the air ringing with decades of the rosary, the bishop's voice piped through loudspeakers rented from Brown's Electrical.

'Aye,' my mother said, and reached for the bunch of gladioli she'd bound into a plastic shopping bag with a rubber band. She slipped the elastic off and placed the flowers on the pebbles, squinting through the smoke as her hands arranged the petals to her satisfaction.

'Some dreams you'll never make head nor tail of,' she said. 'I wouldn't put much pass on it. Anyhow — '

She removed the cigarette from her mouth, examining the indentation above the filter. 'We may get out of here before the people start arriving.'

'We're not staying for the Mass?'

She stubbed the fag out on an upturned

sod, got to her feet and gathered the cleaning stuff.

'No one in their right mind stays in town the day of the Patron.' She pronounced it *Pattern*. 'Once the pubs open people will be tearing scelps out of each other.'

We picked our way between the plots, passing through the shadow thrown by the great grey angel. My mother lowered her voice.

'These goms come to town to pray for their dead,' she said, 'and end up joining 'em.'

Jamey kept sending me letters, but the longer I put off replying the harder it was to write.

I thought of a story he told me about a guy who goes to his physician complaining of weight loss and a bellyache. The doctor refers him to a specialist, who decides they need to operate. When the sawbones opens him up they find sixty feet of tapeworm inextricably entwined with his intestines. They're afraid to remove it in case it starts to thrash about and damage his vital organs. So what do they do? They close him up and send him home and tell him to live with it.

One morning when I got up my mother was wearing her good clothes and her coat was draped over her arm.

'You going somewhere?' I said.

'Visiting.'

'Who?'

'Never you mind. I'll be back to make the dinner. Try and stay out of mischief.'

I sat cross-legged on my bedroom floor and re-read Jamey's most recent letter.

> Balinbagin Boys' Home
> 7 Priory Road
> Balinbagin

Hey John

As you can see from the address, I've been here a week now, and the bizarre thing is, it's not so bad. In fact, it's like Butlins compared to living in the same house as Dee and Maurice. The food's a bit crap and the work is boring and they take your phone away until the weekend, but there's an old prefab out the back where you can sneak a smoke between classes. Most importantly, nobody's tried to bugger me behind the bikeshed.

The staff are all softies. All you have to do is cough ABUSE! and they go running for fear of a solicitor's letter. The other lads are decent enough too. I'm the posh boy. This hard nut called Ger Tarp gave me a bit of a grueller the first week, but when word got round why I was here, he backed off. It didn't hurt to drop Gunter's name either. Turns out word of his exploits has penetrated even the inner sanctum of Balinbagin Boys' Home.

We have to do community service at the weekends, which means raking people's lawns or cleaning up Balinbagin Park, and we went on a sort of goodwill mission to the local mentaller the other day, brought these care packages of toiletries and stuff. That was a laugh and a half.

Weird thing is, I could walk out of here anytime. No big walls with barbed wire or searchlights or tracker dogs or any of that. But to tell you the truth, it wouldn't be worth the hassle. Maurice would frogmarch me straight back in.

Anyway, I've been coming up with loads of stories. There's nothing else to do at night except play cards or watch the telly, and that gets old fairly fast. I've enclosed one — more to follow later. All I ask is you don't show them to anybody else, at least not yet. The reason will become obvious once you read them. I'll get around to changing the names to protect the guilty at a later stage. Meanwhile, store in a safe place. This one's about your friend and mine, Garda Sergeant Jim Canavan, arresting officer in the case of The People versus Me. You might use it as bribe material should he give you more grief. Tell him a little bird named Corboy told you. If I'd known about some of this stuff before the court case, I might have blackmailed the bugger into dropping the charges.

They're talking about letting me out this weekend. To be honest, I think I'd rather stay put — at least until I've had a chance to straighten things out with Gunter. He keeps texting me these wonderful little haiku. YOU'RE DEAD, SNITCH — that kind of thing. It'd be good to see you though, if you have the time. Want to meet up at the train station in Ballo? I'll be on the seven o'clock, Friday evening. I'll buy you a pint, just drop me a line.

Anyway,
Hope all's good on your end.
No danger of a letter I suppose?
Jamey

Free Love

by Jamey Corboy

Jim Canavan shut the front door. Loud music and gunshots and car crash sounds from the living room. He padded quietly to the lounge

179

and eased the door open, thinking maybe he'd catch Conor on the hop with a cigarette, even a joint.

The curtains were drawn across the bay windows. The boy was sprawled on a beanbag. His face flickered in the light of the screen. Baggy jeans, T-shirt three times too big, trainers with laces undone. He wore his hair in brutal military cut and his jaw was fuzzed with beard. Fast becoming a man, big deep voice on him. Scary how fast.

'You keep sitting like that,' Canavan said, 'you're asking for back trouble.'

The boy looked at his father only to roll his red-rimmed eyes. He returned his attention to the shoot-'em-up.

'All right,' Canavan said. 'But don't come whinging to me if you're in a hoop by the time you're thirty. Where's your mum?'

'Out. Her book club.'

A conspiratorial smirk passed between them. He felt the tiniest twinge of guilt as he shut the living-room door.

He climbed the steps to the landing and unlatched the hot-press door and felt the tank under the lagging jacket. The movement reminded him of his courting days, slipping the hand under a girl's shirt, warm skin, fumbling bra-strap catches. The tank was piping hot. He checked the immersion switch. On. All day, probably. Another hole in my pocket, dear Rita.

When the bath was halfway full he stepped in, slowly lowering his body into the hot water. Once submerged, he tensed his stomach muscles and surveyed his chest and belly.

'Not too bad for an old lad,' he said, his voice spookily loud in the small tiled room.

He didn't feel like an old lad. He weighed about the same as the day he was married.

He smoothed his hair back and breathed in the warm bath vapours and sighed. Just like he could have predicted, the feeling came upon him, that unfathomable sadness, like a mourning for something he couldn't put a name on. He cursed this mood, like hangover guilt, but without the benefit of having gotten drunk in the first place.

His hand went to his hard-on.

If he thought about it, he could probably pinpoint the exact day, the exact moment when he decided he was going to cheat on Rita. It was like being off the fags, but the fever of wanting becomes too much and you make a conscious decision to lapse, and your heart pounds as you're walking to the shop with your money in your fist and your hands shake as you shred the plastic and open up the box and stick that bastard cancerstick in your mouth and light it up and fuck the consequences.

He told himself that Rita had cheated on him too, only in a different way. They hadn't slept together since the Christmas party a couple of years ago. They were both drunk. She'd been flirting with Hyland all night, that yappy gobshite. And before that, periods where she hadn't touched him for months on end. He wasn't exactly blameless, he had to admit. He gave up on her. But god, how do you go about asking your wife to put out? It was embarrassing.

So he waited, hoping she'd eventually come around, and then one day he realised he was the only one waiting. He realised that the waiting itself made him accountable, or responsible, or no, what was the word? *Complicit*.

Thing was, he still had feelings for her. OK, she wasn't the same woman as twenty years ago, he wasn't blind. But when he looked in her face she was still the girl he married and danced with that day in the Salt Island Hotel, the day of their wedding. 'Unchained Melody', her choice. Even now, if she'd just make some gesture to let him know she was still interested, he'd respond in a second. He would. But she seemed to just not care. And as much as he told himself it was all right, sex is not that important, you can go without, there are other things in life blah-blah-blah, he wasn't fooling anyone.

Once he'd made up his mind to cheat, there was no going back. He was too excited by his resolution. Women everywhere he looked. Like that time the young one from the hairdresser's got drenched in the rain. Not all that young either, but she was a fine bit of stuff, almost boyish, what do they call it, *gamine*, hair cut short and dyed off her head, she had a body on her, my god, she'd had a couple of babies, twins, he'd seen her pushing them around in one of those double buggies, but she'd made an outstanding recovery.

It was warm that day and she was wearing a short skirt that showed off her legs and she had on a light-green T-shirt and the sudden shower caught her by surprise, she just stood and let herself get wet through like a scene from a film. She had incredible tits. He wondered if she'd had a job done, or maybe she was still breast-feeding. It didn't matter. He had to hurry home to relieve himself.

For weeks after that he was in a sort of fever, balls throbbing, a permanent lump there between his legs. Girls coming out of the bank in their white blouses and sheer tights and high heels, tottering like baby giraffes. Young mothers gathered around the school gate calling out their children's names, generous arses squeezed into immaculate blue jeans or combat trousers or sweat suits that didn't quite obscure their curves. Little teenage things all dolled up for the pub on weekends — why didn't girls dress like that when he was young? Sometimes after closing time he watched them stagger to the takeaway, stocious and coupled at the arm, swaying like stunned heifers.

Then *she* came along. He saw her sitting in the beer garden in Donahue's one night, sipping her vodka and smoking her cigarettes. He'd gone in for a late pint and they got talking. She was impish as hell. He liked that. Before he'd even finished his first pint she kissed him, bold as you like. His body was electrified. The hairs stood up on the back of his hands.

The next morning he was stricken with the guilt. But the guilt went away pretty fast. Or maybe he just got used to it. He thought about people who get married because they fear being lonely. They don't know the meaning of the word. He didn't want to turn into an old man made bitter with regrets. Sometimes he felt like the poor old horse from *Animal Farm*, what was his name,

Boxer. I will work harder, that was the horse's solution for everything. And look where that left you if you weren't careful.

In the bath, with your prick in your hand.

But things had changed.

He'd changed.

The water lapped against his legs. He imagined her head bobbing there, her tongue working wonders on his fatigue, bringing his body back to life. He conjured her touch, the way she kissed, like she was starving, like she might eat the face off him. It was so at odds with her everyday manner, which was sulky and taciturn.

The water had grown tepid. He gripped the sides of the bath, hauled himself out with a groan. Dried off. Went into the bedroom and removed a set of fresh clothes from the wardrobe. Rita had been at him to empty his stuff out so she could have it for her shoes. Seventeen years in this house and he still felt like he didn't fit with the decor, like he was a gaudy heirloom or a bad painting migrating from room to room.

He checked his phone.

One new message. Text.

Come on over. M.

Later, when they were both flushed and spent, he nestled against her bony backside.

She wriggled around to face him.

'Don't be coming near me with your piss-horn,' she said sleepily, and groped between his legs. He closed his eyes and smiled the smile of a satisfied man. She was some piece of work, all right. The way she let herself go while she was lying under him, or straddling him, the way she didn't care.

They nuzzled for a bit and then she propped herself up on elbows, looked in his face.

'Ever think of getting out of here, Jim? We could do it, you know. You could get a transfer or something.'

He clasped his hands behind his head. He reeked of sex-sweat, but she didn't seem to mind. Maggie wasn't the prudish type.

'I couldn't leave Conor,' he said.

'He'd be OK. He's not a child any more.'

She reached for his hand, the gold band on his ring finger.

'I hate that you still sleep with her.'

Here we go.

'I don't *sleep* with her. We share a bed, that's all. We haven't slept together in years.'

'I still hate it.'

'You're not exactly Miss Fidelity yourself.'

She turned away. He wanted to touch her but made himself wait. He wasn't some young lad she could wrap around her finger.

Eventually she broke the silence.

'I just wish I could be with you more. It's the only time I ever feel safe.'

He didn't answer. She slipped her hand between his legs again.

'Will you stay the night? Gunter's out till eight.'

'I'd love to, but I can't. Not tonight.'

She got out of the bed and padded downstairs. He lay on that strange bed and gazed at the ceiling and wondered if at any time in the history of the human race there'd existed such a thing as free love.

The day Jamey was due home, I stood on the main Ballo road with my thumb stuck out and played roulette with the registration plates, trying to make the traffic stop by sheer force of will, but it just whooshed past. Each car that flashed by made me check my watch and pace the hard shoulder, muttering and swearing.

I tucked my hair under my collar and buttoned up my jacket and tried to present the appearance of a respectable human being. And I remembered what Jamey told me that night in the Rugby Club, that it was all about attitude, so I put my shoulders back and stuck my chin out and looked directly into the windscreen of the next car that came along.

A deep red Toyota pulled over about fifty yards up the road.

You beauty.

I trotted after it, but my heart sank when I saw the driver was a woman. It had to be a mistake. Earlier in the afternoon another lady driver had stopped for me and it was awful: I ran towards her car and opened the passenger door and her eyes flew wide open and she shrieked and it turned out she hadn't stopped for me at all, she'd just pulled in to use her phone. I didn't want an action replay, so I stood gawking like a daw, waiting for something to happen.

The Toyota idled on the side of the road. The girl rolled down the window and yelled.

'You coming or not?'

I ran the last few yards and opened the door.

'Miss Ross,' I said.

She smiled, showing bleach-white teeth.

'Thought it was you. I never forget a face. Get in.'

The door clunked shut, sealing the vacuum.

'Sorry, Miss,' I said, arranging my feet. 'I didn't expect to get a lift from a lady driver.'

She checked the rear-view mirror as I clipped the belt on.

'Call me Molly, please. I'm taking a year out from teaching. At least.'

That was news. I always had the impression that teachers did the same thing their whole lives, like nuns or convicts.

'Tell you what,' she said. 'Let's pretend we just met. I'm Molly Ross.' She reached over her small hand and gave my fingers a squeeze. 'And you are?'

I cleared my throat. Felt like maybe I was the butt of some joke.

'John.'

She released my hand and put the car in gear.

'So, John, where you going?'

I looked out the windscreen at the distant clouds, some answer to it all encoded in their inkblot shapes.

'Ballo town.'

She smiled, and it gouged dimples in her cheeks.

'Off to commune with the ocean? Talk to the dolphins?'

'Something like that.'

She brushed hair back from my face. 'There,' she said, and reached for her bag and one-handedly removed a silver cigarette case and a Zippo.

'Smoke?'

She flipped the lighter open, lit me first,

then herself. My mouth felt dry. I'd been smoking too much.

We passed some bollards and crunched across a bed of loose chippings. Miss Ross slowed the car until the road became smooth again. She was wearing a white blouse tucked into a black skirt that stopped just shy of the knee. The hem rode up and down as her fashionable shoes worked the pedals. Up and down. Sheer blue tights. It was very warm. There was a plastic Jesus magnetised to the dashboard. She noticed my stare.

'Kitschy, huh?' she said.

There was nothing kitschy about it.

'So,' she said, stubbing out her cigarette, half smoked. 'Get up to anything interesting over the summer?'

I couldn't even begin.

'Not really.'

Her mouth went wavy-lined.

'You're not giving me much to work with here, John. C'mon.'

'Sorry.'

She returned her attention to the road. We came to a village, not even a village, it didn't have a name, just a strip of buildings: petrol station, pharmacy, one of those mini-markets where you pay at a hatch, like a post office. Molly Ross geared down and pulled in.

'Won't be a sec,' she said, and shouldered open the door and disappeared into the building. A couple of minutes later she reappeared, stuffing something into her handbag. We drove some more. Two-pubs-and-a-shop stops. Roadside nurseries. Cooking apples for sale. Molly Ross flicked the winker on. I looked at her like I was asking a question, but I kept my mouth shut. The car turned off the main road and into the mouth of a narrow laneway. We crunched over gravel until we came to a rickety wooden gate. She parked and turned off the engine.

'Are you all right?' she said.

'Uh-huh.'

My voice was a toad's croak. My shoulders were all knotted. I needed to get to Ballo as soon as possible; it was getting late and Jamey's train would be in soon.

She twisted in her seat and looked directly into my eyes, and my cheeks started to heat up. There was nowhere to look that wasn't her. Her prim face reminded me of the bit in *Harper's Compendium* that explained why people find facial symmetry attractive, because having a face where the two sides are like mirror images is considered a sign of good health and a potential breeding partner. Intestinal parasites made people's features lopsided.

Molly Ross stared at me some more. I stared back. She put her hand on my leg and leaned in close.

'Do you fancy me at all, John?'

I tried to talk, but no words left my mouth, just that gritty throat sound.

'It's OK,' she said. 'You don't have to answer.'

She planted her mouth on mine, and her tongue darted between my lips. Her breath tasted of tic-tacs. Over her shoulder, the plastic Jesus' palms were turned upward in what was probably intended as a gesture of compassion, but in the context it looked as though he was saying *what can you do?*

My throat made a noise; Molly Ross stopped the kissing.

'Are you sure you're OK with this?'

I nodded. She went back to kissing me, more urgently this time, and began to unbutton things. My hands sort of flapped about and my stomach shrank back as her fingers groped and probed places I'd never been touched before in my life, and my heart went gabba-gabba speed-metal double-bass drums and my arms and legs began to shake.

She reached into her bag and fumbled out a box of condoms with a picture of a sailboat on the front, pushed my seat back and climbed on top. I pawed at her blouse and she undid her bra from the front and then hair and braless breasts hung in my face. She fumbled the condom box open, shook one out, tore the wrapping off and pinched the air out of the teat. She pulled me out of my trousers and rolled the rubber on, then tugged her tights and panties down and mounted, guiding me in, moving her weight about.

The smell of us polluted the car. A voice babbled from the back of my brain.

The hookworm has dagger teeth which it uses to gnaw into capillaries and devour the intestine, injecting its host with an anti-clotting agent.

Her backside pistoned.

Or a pinworm. Pinworms are sometimes found in the vulva, the uterus and the fallopian tubes because they get lost on the way back to the anus after depositing their eggs.

She splayed her hands across the dashboard and pranged her lower half onto my pelvic bones.

The South American carnero fish has sharp bones with a series of spines located around the head. It follows urine smells in water and enters swimmers' urethras. It swims up the victim's penis and extends its spines and takes in blood, expanding as it feeds.

Our bodies made slapping noises. The

plastic Jesus watched it all, palms up.

The only cure is an expensive form of surgery that involves inserting the Xagua plant and the Buitach apple up the urethra, which kill and then dissolve the carnero fish. For people who can't afford the operation, amputation is the only cure.

I was on a hair-trigger. I remembered the one Fintan told us about Snow White sitting on Pinocchio's face and moaning tell-a-lie-tell-the-truth-tell-a-lie-tell-the-truth, and that made me even more excited somehow. My own Pinocchio nose seemed to grow longer with each stroke and the feeling came upon me and I let it go, thinking, *I'm a real boy now.*

Molly Ross sensed the shudders and moved up a gear, panting, *fuck-fuck-fuck-fuck*, ramming her hind parts onto my front parts, but I'd already emptied out. I was going rubbery and limp down there, and it hurt a bit.

She stopped moving, carefully reached down and extracted me and climbed off and flopped into the driver's seat.

'Sorry,' I mumbled.

'S'OK.'

She took a packet of wipes from her handbag and dabbed at her undercarriage and pulled her tights back up.

'First time, huh?'

'Yeah.'

I felt strange and sort of sick. I wanted to go home, but it was too late to turn back.

'Never mind,' she said. 'It gets better.'

She unwound the car window, carefully tugged the rubber off of me and threw it into the ditch where it hung from a briar, withered and deflated. Again with the wipes, and she started the engine and manoeuvred the car around. We bumped down the lane and back onto the main road. She tousled my hair. I gave her a weak smile and zipped up my fly and buckled my belt.

'Hey,' she said. 'It's fine.'

The sudden kindness in her voice made my eyes prickle. Silence swallowed everything. I didn't speak again until we'd reached Ballo town. She insisted on running me all the way to the train station, even though it was out of her way.

As I got out, she leaned across the passenger seat and squeezed my arm. All I felt was sad and homesick.

I watched her drive away into the what-was-coming.

The train station was deserted. The digital timetable hanging over the platform said there were no more arrivals due until morning. The sky behind the mountains was beginning to redden up; another couple of hours and the light would fail and with it my chances of getting a lift home. The whole day had been for nothing.

I left the station and walked down the creaking woodenworks under the hulking shadow of a rust-coloured trawler moored to the dock by groaning ropes as thick as jungle vines. Dinghies and dories bumped against the boardwalk's supporting struts. Across the sound, cranes and diggers silhouetted the skyline, and great white storage containers like sinister prefabs glowed yellow under sodium lights.

Disgusted with the world, I lit a cigarette.

Across the street, a car growled into life. It executed a rough U-turn and inched along the kerb. The back window rolled down and Gunter Prunty stuck his big head out.

'Hop in.'

Fintan was in the driver's seat, Davy hunched in the back on the far side. I flicked ash from my cigarette and stared at the tip. The prospect of getting into a car with those three wasn't exactly appealing, but I didn't want to be stranded in Ballo either.

'All right.'

I tossed the cigarette. Gunter shouldered the door open and got out to let me in. Davy shoved over and stared out the window. The car stank of skunkweed and cowshit. Fintan twisted around in his seat.

'Sorry 'bout the squeeze,' he said. 'We're carrying a load.' He patted one of several fertiliser sacks dumped on the front passenger seat and stacked on the floor.

The car pulled onto the road and accelerated out of Ballo. Fintan turned on the car radio and punched the pre-sets. Pop songs and wafts of classical music. Traffic reports. Ads read by people talking faster than auctioneers. Two taps of a stick on a snare drum and a ceilidh combo piled hell for leather into a jig or a reel. Fintan turned it up so loud the sound was distorted. The noise and smoke made me dizzy. I realised I hadn't eaten all day.

We bombed up the main Kilcody road, diddley-eye music blaring. Fintan drove like a lunatic, taking the bends at reckless speed. Occasionally he removed both hands from the wheel to adjust his ponytail, steering with his knees. Gunter lit a joint and passed it to Davy. The reek was foul. Through the windscreen, the broken white line blurred under the front of the bonnet like a tractor beam, reeling us home. The lights of Kilcody appeared in the distance. I willed them closer.

We reached the end of a long straight

stretch of road and came up fast on a hairpin bend. The joint came round to me. I took a couple of drags and passed it over the headrest to Fintan. Eyes locked on the approaching bend, he reached back to take the joint and knocked it from my fingers and it tumbled end over end into his lap, sparks flying. He yelped, and the car swerved all over the road as he clawed between his legs. His elbow jarred the radio's volume switch and the ceilidh music jumped to a deafening level. Headlights flashed. An oncoming car loomed in the windscreen and blazed past us, horn blaring. We skidded around the bend, skimming the far ditch, but somehow managed to stay on the road. Fintan finally located the joint and stuck it in his mouth. He killed the radio and glared over his shoulder.

'You nearly burnt the balls off me, young fella.'

'Never mind that,' Davy said. 'I think that was the squad car.'

'Pull the other one.'

'I'm serious.'

Fintan swivelled around, bug eyed.

'If you're winding me up, I'll throttle you.'

'I think he's right,' Gunter said. 'I thought it was the squadder too.'

Fintan checked the rear-view mirror,

horror spreading across his face like blood from a cut.

'If they catch me I'm screwed,' he said. 'I'm barred from driving. I hope your pal's on duty, Gunter.'

Davy twisted in his seat and peered through the grid of the defrosting panel on the back window.

'Should I ditch the blow?' he said.

'Not yet,' Gunter said, deadpan.

Fintan flicked off the lights and hugged the wheel. He floored the accelerator, nose almost touching the windscreen. The speedometer twitched towards the 70 mark as we hurtled through the twilight.

Just before we reached the outskirts of the village, Fintan turned the lights back on and hung a right out the coast road.

'You can drop me off here,' I said. 'I'm going the other way.'

'We're not stopping anywhere until we get to the slaughterhouse,' Fintan said.

A mile or so down the road we turned onto a grass split lane and clunked over the bars of a cattle grid and onto an expanse of balding waste ground. The old slaughterhouse was little more than a crude shed constructed from mismatched off-cuts of corrugated iron, its rickety roof insulated with a ragged patchwork of felt, the sole window blacked out with ripped plastic sacking. Gorse bushes peeped over a surrounding chicken wire fence.

We waited, ears sharpened against the stillness. No squad car.

Fintan put the handbrake on and boosted the radio. Someone spoke in Irish for a bit and then some old guy began to sing a *sean nós* air. Gunter got out and grabbed one of the fertiliser bags. The other two followed suit, dragging the heavy sacks toward the slaughterhouse door. I made as if to help, but Fintan ordered me to stay put. The *sean nós* singer's dirge droned.

Fintan leaned in and popped the boot.

'C'mere,' he said.

I followed him around the back of the car. He swung the boot open.

Jamey was trussed up like an animal. His body was wedged between the spare wheel and the jack. His mouth was sealed with a strip of electrical tape and his hands were tied with binder twine that chafed his wrists an ugly red. His glasses were crooked on his nose and his eyes bulged like a spooked horse's.

Everything telescoped. I tore the tape from Jamey's mouth and tried to lift him out of the car, but something exploded against the side of my head and my ears whined. Rough hands yanked my arms behind my back and forced me to the ground, face first, my chest crushed against the hard cement. Blood leaked down the back of my throat, the sour tang of iron. Fintan was kneeling on my back and it was hard to breathe.

Gunter loomed over us, tall and silent as a standing stone. He grabbed Jamey by the scruff, hauled him out of the car and paused a moment. He seemed to consider his options.

Davy made limbering up shapes, rolling his shoulders.

'Are we going to do this or what?' he said.

From the car radio, a maudlin violin scraped out some godforsaken air.

Gunter kissed the knuckles of his right hand and swung. The impact sounded like someone cracking a belt. Jamey's head rocked back and his knees gave out. Davy caught him, pinning the arms like he was holding a punchbag. Gunter kept slugging. The dull sickening thuds and gasps and surprised sounds were loud in the calm summer's evening. There was no hurry; that was the worst part. It went on and on until Gunter ran out of steam. Breathing heavily, he placed his hands on his knees, face flushed from the exertion.

'Had enough?' he panted. A drop of sweat

wobbled from the tip of his nose. My neck ached from straining to see what was going on from my vantage point on the ground.

Jamey didn't answer. Blood dribbled down his chin and his lips were all gashed and split. He gobbed a clot of bloody phlegm onto the ground.

'I'll take that as a yes,' Gunter said, and hiked up the leg of his jeans and removed a hunting knife from inside his boot. A shard of fading sunlight refracted off the blade. Jamey's eyes followed it, his Adam's apple moving up and down. Everything went quiet; even the music stopped for a moment. Then, from the car, a girl's voice rang out, pure and unaccompanied.

Black is the colour . . .

Gunter grabbed Jamey's wrists, sawed through the binder twine and quickly stepped away.

'Strip,' he said.

Jamey rubbed his wrists and wiped blood from his face with his sleeve.

'Go fuck yourself,' he said.

Gunter lifted a lock of Jamey's fringe away from his eyes with the blade of the knife.

'Do it. Unless you want a haircut.' He traced a line through the blood and grime, all the way down Jamey's cheek. 'Or a facelift.'

Jamey stayed perfectly still, as though he

hadn't heard a word.

Gunter roared: 'Now!'

Jamey began to take his clothes and runners off with clumsy hands. Gunter kicked the clothes into a pile. He planted his feet apart, unzipped, extracted himself and began to piss on them. Steam rose up, attracting midges. He shuddered as he finished pissing.

'More than three shakes is a sin,' Davy said.

Gunter pulled his fly up.

'Just get in the fucking car, Dave.'

Fintan removed his knee from my back. I tried to push myself up, but he feinted a jab at my head, laughing when I flinched, and glared a moment, as if daring me to make another move. His eyes were cold and soulless, completely blank.

'Come on, Fin,' Gunter snapped.

They took their time getting back into the car. I half expected them to change their minds and come back, but eventually they slammed the car doors and started the engine and roared off through the gateway and across the cattle grid. The engine's sound receded and then there was only a strained, taut silence.

Jamey sank to his haunches, wobbly as a calf. He was pale from shock, and his naked frame looked scrawny and fragile. I shrugged off my jacket and passed him my long lumberjack shirt. He knotted it around his middle with trembling hands. It hung from his waist like a skirt.

'Got any smokes?'

It sounded like he'd had teeth pulled. Took him three matches to light the cigarette.

'I'm sorry,' I said. 'This is my fault.'

'You're sorry?'

He hunkered like a primitive, glowering at the ground between his bare feet for a moment, then looked up at me through the smoke, one eye already closing over.

'Where'd they find you?' he said.

'Outside the train station.'

He nodded.

'Bad luck.'

'Jamey, I have to tell you something.'

He shook his head.

'No you don't.'

He stared hard into my eyes. Maybe Canavan told him. Maybe Gunter. Either way he knew.

He spat on the ground and said, 'It's history, man. Piss in a river.'

And then he stood, wincing a bit.

'Just tell me something,' he said. 'That night in the chapel. What possessed you?'

Slowly I shook my head.

'I don't know. I can't remember any of it. Only what they showed me on the tape.'

Jamey nodded and moved his lower jaw around, as if making sure it was still attached to the rest of his head.

'Well,' he said, 'something happened. You were raving like a loon, man. I thought you'd wake the whole village.'

'Why didn't you stop me?'

'I was kind of in shock. Besides.' He grinned. 'I was getting some good stuff. You threw the chalice at the cross and started going apeshit, knocking over statues and upending the pews and all kinds of stuff. Holy Communion everywhere. Then your face went white. Actually, it was more a kind of green. You spewed all over the altar.'

'They said it was . . . '

'I know. It wasn't. After you puked your guts up, you ran off. I followed you, but I forgot the camcorder. And the tape.'

'I'm sorry.'

Jamey looked me in the eye again.

'It's done.'

Ash fell from the tip of his cigarette. You could feel the whole summer's heat trapped in the ground.

He blew smoke into the air and chuckled.

'Balinbagin was like a holiday home, man. All I did was write. You were the one doing the time. I heard you were miserable. I was kind of touched.'

He flicked his cigarette away.

'Y'know, I was waiting for this all summer. Dreading it. Now it's done.'

'How did you know what was going to happen?' I said.

He bent over the pile of piss-sodden clothes and took money and keys from his jeans.

'Because it happened before,' he said. 'Gunter told me.'

He reached inside his jacket and removed a folded sheaf of papers from his jacket.

'Here,' he said, and thrust them at me. 'Read this when you get home.'

The papers were damp in parts, but still legible. I stuffed them into my back pocket.

Jamey stuck his hand out. I shook it without quite knowing why.

'Look after yourself,' he said and began to move stiffly across the yard.

'Where you going?' I said.

'Away. Don't tell Dee anything. Just play dumb, no matter how freaked out she gets. I'll call her as soon as I can.'

He walked slowly across the cattle grid. Before he disappeared into the evening light, he called out: 'I'll send a postcard.'

Then he disappeared, and all I had left of him were stories.

The old crow knows the story. He sees it all unfold like a sequence of silent irised images. Figures move in herky-jerky movements, but no matter what happens he does not intervene, for in his starved bird mind all mortal events are merely dreams of what happens. Even a crow knows that in dreams you cannot change a thing but merely watch with a detachment that is at once benign and malign, like a bored god, or a bored god's messenger.

8

My mother was in bed by the time I got home. I was so tired and sore I couldn't make it up the stairs so I collapsed into her armchair and took Jamey's papers from my back pocket. They smelled and I had to carefully peel the sheets apart to read them. And maybe it was shock, but as I read his words I didn't know whether I should laugh or cry or both.

Balinbagin Boys' Home
7 Priory Road
Balinbagin

John,
I wasn't going to write (it's hard to be bothered when the correspondence is all one way) but the weirdest thing happened. Your mother came to see me this morning. She asked me not to let on, but you know me, can't keep my trap shut. I thought maybe she'd be fishing for information about a certain person's involvement in you-know-what, but the subject never came up. She just asked if they were feeding me and if I was keeping out of trouble. She

stayed about half an hour and listened to me yammering on and then she left. I still don't know what to make of it.

Anyway, seeing as I'm writing, I might as well send you my latest story. The stuff's pouring out of me these days — must be the artist-friendly environment. I hope you're keeping them in a safe place, they might be worth money someday.

Talk soon.

JC

The Cuckold

by Jamey Corboy

Gunter Prunty was a big man, and not easily intimidated. As a schoolboy, he was able to whale the crap out of boys three or four years older and not think twice about it. Even the teachers were a little scared of him. But one thing Gunter dreaded more than anything was being asked to stand up in English class to read aloud. It reduced him, a giant of a lad, to a stuttering red-faced mess.

Gunter was not what you'd call a man of letters. He'd never read a book in his life. And yet, at the grand old age of twenty-seven, poorly schooled, having failed to complete his Leaving Cert, he became fixated on a word he'd heard somewhere. Not your everyday word either. It stuck in his brain like a fishhook.

Cuckold.

Maybe he'd heard it on the telly or in a film. He wasn't a hundred per cent on the meaning, but he definitely had a hunch it pertained to what had been going on with him and Maggie, so one night in Donahue's he asked the Corboy lad, who fancied himself a bit of a scholar. When Corboy told him, Gunter figured they might as well have printed his mug shot where the word appeared in the dictionary.

Cuckold.

He could almost taste it. He tongued it like a bad tooth. Pronounced it different ways. Played charades with it.

Cuckold.

Sounds like: Cock-holed. Butt-plugged by another man in a three-way pile-up. A fuck sandwich, with Maggie as the filling.

That girl had his heart scalded, no two ways about it.

Cuckolded.

Now it sounded kind of chickeny.

Buk-awk-buk-buk.

The weird thing was, deep down, in some secret, dirty place he could barely bring himself to acknowledge, Gunter was *excited* by her carry on, because anything was better than being bored, and most of the time, he and Maggie bored each other stupid. Yes, jealousy festered inside him like an ulcer, inflamed him with rage. But at the same time, the thought of her with another man sent an illicit shiver through his mind. Sometimes he lay in bed pulling the guts out of himself, imagining her face contorted with pleasure as she writhed under some gurning punter. But always afterwards, his ejaculate hardening to a crust, he felt pathetic and ashamed.

The very first night they met, she was fresh off the boat from England, with no plans to go back. 'I've had enough of bastards,' she told him when the drink had loosened her tongue. 'Handsome bastards. Ugly bastards. Hard bastards. Soft bastards. My whole life, bastards. I must give off some smell that attracts them.'

Gunter too could be a bastard if it suited, but when it came to Maggie he was a soft touch, even when she threw things at him, or pummelled him with her fists and he had to thrust his hands in his pockets to keep from hitting back. Even when she started coming home late smelling of Donahue's.

One such night when she crawled into bed, instead of letting him mount her, she put her hand on his head and gently but firmly pushed him down between her thighs. Gunter was a little shocked and unsure about how to proceed, but he gave it a shot, burrowing into her coarse hair, her woman-smell. At first she squirmed and groaned and made whimpering noises, and he took this as encouragement. He stayed down there for ages, tongue sore and strained, her moistness tingling his cheeks. But when at last he lifted his head, she'd fallen asleep.

Try as he might, Gunter couldn't quite pinpoint when he first suspected something dodgy going on. It was just an instinct, a hunch. Sometimes when he kissed her on the mouth, he found himself wondering what she'd had in there lately.

But even when the late nights became more frequent, and his suspicion turned to certainty, he was reluctant to confront her. He was kind of curious as to how the thing would play out. He waited up late in the kitchen, lights out, downing shots of whiskey, trying to quench that giddy sick feeling in his stomach. He grew addicted to that feeling, addicted to quenching it. He drank and smoked and drank and smoked and relieved himself against the backyard wall and asked the rain what's the fucking point, but the rain didn't know a thing, just hissed and plonked.

He lay awake in bed at night listening for

the sound of her stealing in like a stray. He pretended to be asleep when she crept into the bedroom, and just when she thought she'd gotten away with it, he'd speak, his loud voice in the darkness, making her start. He'd ask where she'd been, not because he wanted to know the truth, but because he wanted to hear her recite the lies she'd prepared.

Then he took to going through her coat and bag on the sly. He scrolled through her text messages when she was asleep or in the bath. He snooped around the bedroom. And when he found proof, it was in a place so obvious he had to wonder if she wanted to be caught. A Durex box stashed at the bottom of the drawer where she kept her underwear. Gunter never used rubbers. Like eating through a muzzle, he always said.

He shook the johnnies onto the bedspread, hands trembling, a sour metallic taste in his mouth. Out of a box of twelve, eight left. He paced the flat, sickened and exhilarated. He poured himself a generous measure of whiskey and sat trying to remember, working out the times, the dates, trying to figure out what he'd been doing while she was out fucking this mystery man. At work maybe. Or cleaning the flat when she was too tired or browned off to do it herself. Bleaching the bath, scrubbing the toilet, wearing those

Marigold gloves. Eating takeaways in front of the television because she'd stopped cooking, trying to bury that awful gut feeling under comfort food. Steak and kidney pie. Batter-burgers and chips. Chicken dippers.

Buk-awk-buk-buk.

He was pouring his third whiskey when he heard the key in the door. His stomach flip-flopped. Maggie came into the kitchen, did a double take when she saw the bottle.

'Bit early for that, isn't it?'

He pushed the bottle away.

'Tell me his name.'

She plugged in the kettle.

'Whose name?'

'His name, Maggie. I found the rubbers.'

She folded her arms.

'Gunter, are you off your trolley?'

'The rubbers. In your fuckin' *dresser.*'

She tried to change the subject, demanding to know what he was doing going through her things. She tried to make out the rubbers were her friend June's, but he cut her off, roaring, '*Don't try to make me into a bigger gom than I already am!*' and she burst into tears, but the waterworks only made him madder. He looked at his hands. They were trembling like the morning-after shakes. He tried to get himself under control, tried to swallow his anger, felt it burn all the way

215

down to his stomach. He looked at Maggie, her face crumpled, her bottom lip curling like a child's. He made himself go to her and put his arm around her and be a man.

'Tell me his name,' he said softly.

She shook her head.

'I can't, Gunter. Please stop it.'

'You're only making things worse.'

'Stop.'

But he wouldn't quit. He kept at it until he wore her down.

'If I tell you,' she said, wiping her face with her sleeve, 'do you promise not to do anything?'

Gunter put his big hands on her shoulders.

'I promise.'

'Please, Gunter. I'd be mortified.'

'I swear. Now tell me.'

She swallowed. Looked at the floor.

'Jude.'

'Jude what?'

'Udechukwu.'

He was flabbergasted.

'What in the hell kind of name is that?'

She rubbed her eyes with the heels of her hands. Her mascara was coal-smudged.

'Nigerian.' She buried her face in her hands. 'I'm sorry.'

It came out muffled.

Gunter sat down heavily, like he'd been hit

hard in the gut. *So this is what it's like when someone breaks your heart*, he thought. *You feel it in your stomach, not your chest. You want to throw up.*

The whiskey tasted bitter in his mouth and he felt so dizzy he thought he might collapse. He put his hand on the table to steady himself.

'Sit,' he said, as though giving orders to a dog. He went to the cupboard and took out a second tumbler, dumped whiskey in, pushed it towards her.

'We're not done talking.'

She knocked it back.

He poured a refill. Anaesthetic.

'I want details.'

'Details?'

Her look was withering, but her voice betrayed a tremor.

'Everything.' He took her phone out of her bag and turned it off. 'Every. Last. Thing.'

And he started in with more questions. He wouldn't stop, not until he knew every pornographic fact. The answers hurt, but still he had to find out.

Who else knows?

When was the first time you kissed?

Did he use the tongue?

How deep?

Show me. Use your finger.

Did you undress in front of him, or did you make him turn off the light the way you make me?

Did you make noises while you were doing it?

What kind of noises? Make them now.

Did he put it in by himself or did you put it in for him?

Did you take him in your mouth?

Did he come?

Did you gag?

Spit?

Or swallow?

Was it bigger than mine?

It went on and on until she broke down and swore on her mother's grave that she'd never see the boy again. Gunter waved her away, disgusted, and she fled to the bedroom.

He called Fintan and Davy and told them to meet up in Donahue's.

'First thing,' Gunter told them, 'find out where he drinks. Then report back to me. I don't just want to hurt this prick. I want to fuck with his head too.'

Fintan sniggered as he got up to leave.

'Udechukwu,' he said. 'What a name.'

They left Gunter at the bar thinking ugly thoughts, all of which could've been reduced to a single name repeated like a mantra as he worked himself up into a state.

Udechukwu, Udechukwu, Udechukwu . . .

Two days later, when Jude Udechukwu showed up for work at the petrol station, he went to his locker, as he always did, to change into his overalls. The locker door swung open when he grasped the handle. Inside was a chicken's foot, caked with blood.

Over the next couple of days, Gunter and Maggie tiptoed around each other, picking their way through unfamiliar territory. They both avoided the subject of her indiscretions, afraid it might blow up into a row neither of them had the stomach for. Maggie spent most of her time asleep. If she stayed in that scratcher much longer, Gunter figured, she'd get bedsores. Dirty dishes stacked up in the sink. There was nothing to eat. He was pouring stale cornflakes into a small saucepan when his phone went off. Davy, ringing from Donahue's.

'Looks like he didn't take the hint,' said Davy. 'He's here, all on his tod. I don't know what she sees in him. He ain't the size of a gnat.'

Gunter told him what to do and hung up.

Maggie padded in, still wearing her slob clothes, a baggy hoodie and a pair of leggings.

'Who was that?'

Gunter stepped on the bin pedal and dumped cornflakes into the smelly liner bag.

'Davy.' He put the saucepan on top of the crockery heap. 'I'm going to meet him for one in Donahue's.'

'OK.'

'Fucking right it is.'

Maggie flinched like she'd been slapped, like she might turn on the waterworks again. Gunter turned his back to her, put on his jacket and went outside. He kick-started the bike and roared off, down the old beach road towards the abandoned slaughterhouse.

They beat the lard out of him. Beat him until he shrieked, protesting his innocence the whole time, but they ignored his squeals and went about the business of hurting him like it was a job of work. At some point, Gunter realised his bone was hard and he wanted to stop and go away and figure out what that meant, but the boys kept egging him on and he couldn't lose face so he kept driving his steel-capped boots into the boy's ribs until he was a broken heap sobbing on the ground.

Gunter woke with his knuckles swollen and one of the buckles on his motorcycle boots torn off, but somehow he felt more solid in his centre. That awful churning feeling was gone. So was the disturbing boner. All day long he turned jobs on the lathe, a satisfying ache in his muscles. Even the girls in the office remarked on his good mood. 'Jazes, Gunter, you must be getting some,' remarked the cute young Cullen one in passing.

When he got home, the squad car was parked outside the flat. Jim Canavan was leaning on the roof, smoking one of those cheap skinny cigars. Gunter dismounted and dragged the bike onto its stand.

'Jim.'

'Hop in,' Canavan said, got behind the wheel and sprung the passenger door. Gunter squeezed his bulk into the car and adjusted the seat. Whoever had been sitting there last was a midget.

'You know why I'm here,' Canavan said.

'I've a fair idea.'

'Thing is, he's gone and filed a complaint.'

Gunter nodded.

'I'll come down to the barracks.'

'No need.'

'Ah?'

Gunter raised an eyebrow.

'I'll take care of it,' Canavan said. 'But might want to think ahead next time you decide to hammer the hell out of some young lad, Gunter. You keep fucking up, I keep bailing you out. I'm not careful, you'll cost me my pension. This is the last time.'

He twisted the key in the ignition. Gunter opened the door and got out.

Maggie was lying on the couch under her duvet. Her eyes were red and swollen. Gunter sat on the arm of the chair and put his hand on her head. She pulled away.

'You promised you wouldn't do anything,' she said.

Gunter shrugged.

'I changed my mind.'

She got up and went into the bedroom, dragging the duvet behind like a bloated wedding train.

'You're just like the rest of them,' she said. 'A bastard.'

I stuffed the papers into my jeans, closed my eyes and tried to block out the throbbing in my head. All night I dozed in my mother's armchair until the birds woke me. Disjointed images, dream residue, seeped into the dawn light. My mother came downstairs. With every footstep my heart beat faster.

'Jesus, Mary and *Joseph*,' she said, hand covering her mouth as she stood in the kitchen doorway. 'Were you in a fight?'

'I wouldn't call it that.'

My teeth didn't seem to fit together any

more and my face felt like rubber. She fussed around, poking my ribs and pawing at my scalp and moving my arms like I was a doll or an action man. I told her some story about three total strangers jumping me on the street. She closed her eyes as if waiting for a migraine to pass.

'Whoever they were,' she said, 'they were amateurs. The head is the hardest part of the body. If they wanted to do real damage, they'd have gone for your ribs.'

It didn't feel like an amateur job to me. I was about to say as much but the phone cut me off. My mother frowned.

'Who in the name of god is ringing this early?' She twisted the ends of her hair around smoke-browned fingers. 'Will you get it?'

It was Jamey's mother, almost hysterical, speaking so fast I thought I'd faint from the intensity.

'I've been up all night,' she said. 'Jamey was due home yesterday evening but he never showed. Have you heard anything?'

I told her me and Jamey hadn't spoken in weeks.

'Oh lord,' she said, 'I was hoping you'd seen him.'

My mother hovered over my shoulder and mouthed, 'Who-is-it?' but I waved her away and turned my back.

'If you hear anything,' Dee was saying, 'call me, please. No matter what.'

Her voice started to crack as she thanked me and hung up.

'Well?' my mother said.

'It was Mrs Corboy.'

'What did she want?'

'Jamey's gone AWOL. She wanted to know if I'd seen him.'

She narrowed her eyes.

'And have you?'

'I haven't seen Jamey since his exams finished.'

She lit a cigarette. The nurse in the clinic always gave out to her for smoking before breakfast. Always put something in your stomach first, she nagged.

'I'm sure he'll turn up,' my mother said.

I crawled upstairs to bed and didn't wake until midday, nauseous with hunger.

The holidays moved inexorably towards their end. My face came up in bruises and I barely left the house for fear of running into Gunter and his cronies. One morning I came downstairs and my mother was at the kitchen table, unwrapping tinfoil from a cake.

'The dead arose and appeared to many,' she said. 'Look. Mrs Nagle sent us a barnbrack. She wants to make the peace.'

'She'll never learn.'

'Nor will I.'

She put the cake in the fridge and made a cup of tea and stood at the back door gazing out.

'That's the last of the summer,' she said, squinting at the sun, a watery orb suspended in the sky. 'We should make the best of it. C'mon, I'll pack a lunch and we'll rent a couple of bikes from Tyrell's and go to the beach. The exercise will do us good.'

I got dressed while she made sandwiches and packed them into a wicker picnic basket. She instructed me to fetch a blanket from the press and began unplugging stuff and locking up the house and then she shooed me out the door.

We walked into the village and collected the bikes from Tyrell's. My mother sat up on the saddle and smoked one last fag and then we set off out the old beach road. We had to dismount and walk the bikes up the steep gradient of the hills, but once over the crest we could freewheel for ages. The breeze in our faces made everything feel fresh, a relief from the muggy August heat. We made good time, and soon enough the roads grew narrower and the air was coarse with salt and specks of windblown sand.

Gulls swooped and dived and fought the sea breeze. The fields seemed to draw back, blazing yellow. We heard the tide before we saw it, and as we crested the final hill it was like a blind flew up and the sea yawned wide and the feeling was almost vertiginous.

We hid the bikes in the reeds and strode down the sandy slope. Waves roared and foamed and dashed themselves against the strand. We walked for ages, venturing further down the coast than I'd ever been before. It felt as though we were travelling back in time, pioneers in an unpeopled world. We had to pause every so often while my mother got her breath.

At last we came to a deserted horseshoe-shaped inlet. There was a cave eaten into the cliff face, its jagged overbite about head height, the jaws crammed with rock deposits shaped like fangs, coated with moss and oddly shaped barnacles. Midges and flies buzzed about the beached starfish and stringy clumps of seaweed. My mother took the blanket from me and spread it under the arch of the cave mouth where there was shelter from the sun and wind.

'What is this place?' I said.

'Blowhole Cove.'

It was eerily quiet. My mother settled

herself on the blanket and unpacked the basket. She unscrewed the cap off the flask and gazed out across St George's Channel and watched birds shriek and dive-bomb the water. Herons and gulls prospected for lugworms, picking their steps prissily across the dun sandbars of the sloblands.

'Y'know,' she said, pouring tea into the cap, 'when I was a girl, we came to see a turlhyde whale that washed up right here in this very spot.'

She paused to blow on her tea.

'The boss — that was what we called my father — the boss was usually very strict, but he allowed we'd never see a thing like that again, so he gave us the day off. I'll never forget it.'

My mother hardly ever mentioned her family. I wondered why she was bringing them up now.

'How did the whale end up here?'

'I suppose it strayed into the shallows. Maybe it came here to die.'

Drops of brine blew in off the grey waves, freckling my face. The reek of rotten kelp flooded my nose and throat. My mother passed me a sandwich.

'The old people used to say that anywhere there's a cave near open water is a hell door or a passageway to purgatory.

Or the faerie world. They're all over the country. The Cave of Cruachan by Lough Derg is another one. I bet you don't know how that place got its name.'

I didn't answer, so she went on.

'Lough Derg means 'red lake'. The story goes that when Fionn Mac Cumhaill was fleeing Ulster, he took his mother with him on his shoulders, but he ran so fast that by the time he reached Lough Derg there was nothing left except for her two legs, which he threw down on the ground. When some of the Fianna came looking for him, they found his mother's shin bones and a worm in one of them. They flung the worm in the lake, and it turned into a huge sea monster. Years later St Patrick came and killed it, and the lake ran red with its blood.'

She closed her eyes and let the cold sun bathe her face. Streaks of grey in her hair glittered like highlights.

'I tell you lads,' she said, sounding like she'd been placed in a trance, 'I could fall asleep here.'

The wind picked up, and from far back in the cave's throat came a wailing sound, long-voweled and uncanny, like a banshee's keening.

'What's that noise?' I said.

'Whisht.'

We listened to that mournful drone until the wind died down and the sound subsided.

'That's the blowhole,' she said.

And nodded, agreeing with herself.

The old crow wings high over the dream-scape, omnipotent yet impotent, a doting god who can hear but not respond to the bleating of the afflicted and bereft and the bad luck saps venting at their maker, howling from hilltops at the void, shouting, If you made the world Lord, how could you allow this to happen, all the time overlooking the possibility that He may not be able to do anything about it, that maybe He is just some crow who got struck by lightning and lucked out and created the universe by cosmic fluke, some jammy big bang, and maybe, just maybe, He bailed when things got out of hand, this God-like crow, this crow-like God, perpetually stuck on the other side of things, capable only of observing, whispering hints to the ears of the living but doing nothing of import, omnipotent but impotent.

Is God dead?

Are the dead God?

Don't answer that.

You'll wake the worms.

9

The year's wheel turned, the weather with it. Cold winds came and stripped the trees of leaves and left the branches clawing at the cruel sky like the pincers of lobsters. Blackbirds and jackdaws cawed in the fields; swollen clouds gathered over the mountains; even the sun itself seemed to cast darkness and the sky was a tarpaulin hung so low you could almost reach up and touch it.

It was my Junior Cert year. My mother said that was a good thing — all the extra work would keep me out of trouble. It was still dark when I left for school in the mornings. All day was spent in the fluorescent indoors and by going-home time the darkness had already begun to fall again. I missed Jamey's letters almost as much as his presence.

Sometimes I had imaginary conversations with him, but I couldn't replicate his tone of voice or turn of phrase, and one day I was mildly shocked to realise that I could no longer conjure a clear picture of his face.

I spent the long autumn evenings hatching the fire in our kitchen, a draught at my back, stirring out only to get more firewood from the yard. A patchy scrub of beard grew all over my face and hair crawled down my back. It seemed as though our house had become infested with the ghosts of unspoken things. Silence hung heavy between my mother and me. She shrank into her shadow until her shadow seemed like the most substantial part of her form. She grew paler and frailer and stopped taking her meals at the dinner table and stood over the draining board drinking cups of tea and eating only the odd cut of bread and smoking one cigarette off the last. Every night she was in bed by the nine o'clock news on the wireless, then eight, then straight after dinner.

After she'd gone up I sat abstracted, listening to the rain lashing the windows, wind moaning down the chimney. The sacred-heart lamp cast its blood-red light. Haircut Charlie was bald now; neither of us had sown the seeds of his hair in years. I acknowledged the complaints of our old house, the groaning floorboards and creaking rafters, and looked out the windows at the emaciated limbs of dead trees.

Sometimes I'd go to the cupboard where she kept bottles of spirits for cooking, and I'd siphon some of the liquid into a glass and slowly sip. I liked the effect, the way everything seemed slightly hazy around the edges, the way the drink dulled worry and transformed the world into a place that seemed more careless and full of possibility.

That October my mother was stricken with some sort of bug and took to the bed. I did my best to look after her, but she was the world's worst patient, insisted on trying to get up and go to work before she'd had a chance to recover properly. I told her she'd be better off letting me take charge of things while she recuperated, but she wouldn't hear of it, wouldn't even let me call her GP.

'I'm not paying sixty quid for that doddery old sawbones to tell me to stay in bed and drink plenty of fluids,' she said.

But when a couple of weeks had passed and still no improvement she finally let me send for Dr Orpen. I came home from school one afternoon to find his car parked outside our gate, and I waited at the kitchen table, trying to decipher the murmurs coming from the bedroom.

'The man of the house,' he said when he finally came downstairs.

'What's the news?'

'To tell you the god's honest truth, John, I'm not entirely sure. I don't think it's any one thing. She seems very run down. Has she been eating properly?'

'She was never a big feeder.'

'Well, there isn't a pick on her. She's certainly in no fit state to work. Do you have any relatives that could help out while she's off her feet?'

It was hard to take this in. My mother wasn't the sort of person who got sick for long. Even when she went into hospital for her operation, she recovered in no time.

'I can take care of her,' I said.

Dr Orpen pushed fingers through his steel-wool hair.

'With the best will in the world, John, I don't think you can. She's not a young woman, and she hasn't been looking after herself. Not for a long time, by the looks of it. You'll need help. For the duration anyway.'

Something buzzed in his jacket. He unclipped a pager from his inside pocket, frowned at the display.

'Can I use your phone?'

He spoke for a few minutes and then hung up.

'I have to run,' he said. 'Dan Patterson caught his hand in a mangler.' He grabbed his bag and coat. 'Make sure your mother stays in bed. See if she'll eat something. And for heaven's sake, get her to cut down on the fags.'

I watched him drive away and sat on the front step a moment and lit up, but the smoke gave no succour, only reminded me of my mother's sickness, so I doused it and brushed my teeth and went upstairs to her room. She was dozing, her arms by her side like the withered boughs on the trees surrounding our house. Her skin was grey, her hair lank on the pillow. She opened her eyes when she felt my weight on the edge of the bed.

'How you feeling?' I said.

She tried to smile.

'Weak as a kitten.'

It felt awkward, almost embarrassing, her being sick, me trying to assume the role of carer. I patted her arm.

'I'll let you rest.'

She nodded and closed her eyes.

I sat at the kitchen table and stared out the window at the darkness creeping across the pale winter sky.

That afternoon the back door swung open and the tranquillity of the house was shattered by a voice as loud as a trumpet.

'God save all here!'

Mrs Nagle stood on the threshold like some wild woman of the woods in her furry boots and overcoat and woolly hat. She looked stronger and more robust than I'd ever seen her, like age had bolstered rather than sapped her strength, a powerful cut of a woman who wasn't in the mood to brook any argument from a no-good little *canat* like me. She placed her bags inside the door.

'I'm here to do my bit,' she said, making herself at home in the kitchen, like it had only been a matter of days since her last visit.

'Shhh,' I said. 'She's above in the bed trying to sleep.'

'We have work to do, John.' Her version of a whisper was almost comical. 'We're going to have to pull together, you and me, for your mother's sake.'

She began by making herself a mug of tea and drinking the lot in one lusty gulp. Then she set about organising the place, issuing orders like a sergeant major: we may clean this; we may scrub that. She made out a shopping list in capital letters on the back on an envelope — a loaf of bread and a bag of spuds and two big boxes of Roses — and sent me into the village with a twenty-quid note. When I arrived back, every window in the house was open. I deposited the shopping bags on the kitchen table.

'Change,' she said, holding out her callused talon of a hand.

I placed the coppers on the table and went

upstairs. My mother was awake, propped up by pillows.

'I see Willy Wonka's back,' she said.

For a moment I thought she was romancing, or feverish.

'Willy Wonka?'

'The chocolate factory.'

The curtains billowed in the breeze. I closed the window.

'Is that all right by you?'

She nodded.

'You could use the help. And Phyllis isn't the worst. Just be warned. She'd live in your ear.'

My mother insisted I go to Mass every Sunday. There was no point in upsetting her so I pretended to go, but I didn't have the gall to show my face inside the chapel in case the holy-water font sizzled or I'd be struck by a lightning bolt, so I lurked around the chapel grounds until the service was over.

When the doors opened and the congregation spilled out, I saw Jamey's mother among the crowd. She'd changed her appearance since last time I'd seen her, hair cut into a chic bob, walking arm in arm with Ollie. The boy was getting big; you could tell he was going to grow up into a real bruiser. He spotted me and called out my name and drove his fist into his chest. Dee frowned, followed his pointing finger. Her eyes lit up. She hurried over and squeezed my hand.

'John,' she said. 'How've you been? You look different.'

'I do?'

'Older.'

She clasped my shoulders and held me at arms' length, inspecting my face.

'It's the beard.'

She tugged on the chin bristles.

'Suits you.'

Embarrassed, I blurted the first thing that came into my head.

'Any word from Jamey?' I said.

She put her finger to her lips and tipped her head at Ollie, but it was too late.

'Jamey's on holidays,' Ollie said, and his lower lip quivered.

'We got a postcard,' Dee said breezily. 'And a present. Didn't we, Ollie?'

Ollie nodded and scratched his belly.

'Beanie Babies,' he said.

Dee swept hair out of his eyes.

'Go play.'

Ollie legged it over to the grass. I thought it best to change the subject.

'So what are you doing up here? I thought you'd moved back to Ballo.'

'We did. I don't like the church down

there. It's too big and impersonal. Besides . . . '
She fixed me with her green eyes. 'I'm not
afraid to show my face in there.'

Ollie was rolling around in the grass like a
dog. Dee gazed at him for a moment, turned
to me.

'I think he's in Spain,' she said. 'And I
think there's a girl involved.'

'Really? What makes you say that?'

She shrugged.

'I'm his mother.'

Whatever Dee wanted to believe was fine
by me. Just so long as she didn't start asking
awkward questions. I didn't like lying to her,
not even for Jamey.

'I miss the little smart alec,' she said, and
her expression turned fierce. 'You know what
though? I'm glad he got away from here. I
never wanted him to go to that awful boys'
home. He's a good kid. I wanted to give him
every penny we had in the bank and tell him
to skip the country. But his father wouldn't
hear of it.'

Her face wrinkled with disgust, which gave
way to a sly smile.

'You must think I'm awful.'

'I'm sure any mother would feel the same.'

'You're very kind.' She hugged me, and her
perfume made my head swim. She gave my
arm a squeeze.

'You take care, John.'

And she cupped her hands against her mouth.

'Ollie!'

The boy came running. She held out her hand, but he ignored it and tugged on my shirt. I bent down to his head level and he put his mouth to my ear.

'Cuckoo,' he said into my ear. I could smell crisps on his breath.

'What?'

He grinned and tapped his nose.

'Cuckoo.'

Having Mrs Nagle around to keep an eye on my mother freed me up a bit, but the house was no longer ours. Everywhere reeked of her rotten fruit and fly-spray stench. Her big loud voice shook the dust from the rafters. She made the kitchen into her nest, hanging girdles and tights and all kinds of old lady garments on the clothes-horse by the fire. The fridge was permanently stocked with boxes of chocolates, but I was forbidden to touch them. Her dentures floated in a glass of water placed on the kitchen sink. Dinner was served on the dot of six every evening as the Angelus struck on the wireless. It still tasted burnt.

The only time Mrs Nagle left the house was to get Mass. At night she sat by the fire and stuffed her face with sweets and complained bitterly about there being no television in the house. She slept in the armchair under a quilt, head thrown back, nose in the air, wind whistling through her sinuses, but after a while she complained of her back and took to slipping into bed beside my mother.

'You wouldn't have an old woman sleeping in an old armchair, would you, John?' she said. 'Hah?'

I was exasperated. I'd never met such a bossy woman. It took all my effort to meet her flinty eyes when she spoke, and her voice set my teeth on edge. I couldn't bear her eating noises, the way she chewed with her mouth open, the rasping sound as she scrunched up sweet wrappers and put them in her pocket. Sometimes I wished she'd choke on one of her chocolates, or have a heart attack mid-snore. I fantasised about stuffing a sock in her mouth while she slept and watching her face turn blue.

My mother had rallied a bit by the end of October. She sat up in bed and began to eat a little. Rather than being pleased, Mrs Nagle was noticeably put out. She'd gotten used to running things her own way. The better my mother felt, the more Mrs Nagle fussed around her, keeping me at bay, as if determined to prove how indispensable she'd become to the upkeep of the household. Saucepans constantly boiled on the cooker and the presses were kept stocked, all out of her own pocket, she wouldn't accept so much as the price of a box of teabags. And she had the legs run off me doing messages.

When the weather suddenly turned stormy, blustery winds that rattled the windows and whistled through the eaves, it was with great reluctance that she left to check everything was battened down in her cottage. After she'd gone I sat by my mother's bed, homework spread across my lap, but I'd barely gotten started when the power went out. My mother instructed me to get out the old paraffin-oil lamp from the cupboard under the stairs and showed me how to put a match to the wick without blowing us all up. I screwed the glass chimney in place and set it on the bedside locker and twiddled the knobs until the flame grew tall, creating a magic shadow show on the bedroom wall.

My mother stared at those shadows, and the ghost of a smile played across her face.

'I never told you about the time I saw a giant,' she said quietly.

I put my homework aside. I'd missed her stories.

'Go on.'

'You were still only a scut.' Her voice was faint, but her eyes bright. 'It was a getting dark one evening, I was coming home from work and I saw a shape coming up the road towards me. It was about ten or twelve feet tall, like one of the Tuatha De Danaan. The closer it came, the more anxious I got. My boots were stuck to the road; I was like a scared little rabbit. Then I saw what it was, and I felt like such a gom.'

'What was it?' I said. 'Put me out of my misery.'

She chuckled a little.

'It was two giants, one of them sitting on the other's shoulders.'

My birthday fell on the day before Halloween. My mother was well enough in herself to come downstairs and take her meal at the dinner table. It was the first time she'd been out of bed in weeks, and even though her breath rattled and her movements were so slow it was hard to look at, her spirits seemed improved somewhat.

'Not so sweet sixteen,' she said and winked when she sat down to dinner. She managed to eat most of a plate of watery colcannon and even indulged in a bowl of ice-cream for dessert. Mrs Nagle bustled around the kitchen in a sullen fury, muttering about how a woman in her state should be in bed. My mother threw her a filthy look, and Mrs Nagle's mood abruptly improved.

'Sure what kind of birthday party is this at all?' she exclaimed. 'Let me pop down to the cottage and see what I can find.'

She returned a few minutes later with a box of chocolates and a set of Christmas crackers.

'Now,' she said with forced heartiness. 'This is more like it.'

We ate the chocolates, Mrs Nagle flinching every time I took one. My mother was so weak she could barely pull a cracker, but she placed an orange paper party hat on her head and forced a smile. Mrs Nagle cleared the dinner things away and began the washing-up, and my mother asked me to take her back upstairs. After I'd helped her into bed, she instructed me to open the top drawer of the bedside locker.

'Now,' she said, her voice barely audible, 'take twenty quid from my purse. I want you to go out tonight and have a bit of fun.'

I began to protest, but she wouldn't hear it.

'It's your birthday for heaven's sake. You've

been stuck in this house for weeks with only a pair of old women for company. Go out and have a drink on your mother. Not too many, mind. Phyllis will look after me. Let her earn her keep.'

The prospect of a night out was too tempting to refuse. I waited until my mother was settled and went downstairs and put my coat on. Mrs Nagle was up to her elbows in suds.

'Where are you off to at this hour?' she said.

'Out.'

The village was alive with Halloween sounds and smells, bonfires and smoke, bangers like pistol shots. Packs of children roamed the square, ecstatic with the dark, yelling *trick or treat*. I bought a naggin of whiskey from Hyland's off-licence and sat on the monument and took it all in, alcohol spreading outwards from my stomach to my fingertips.

A car pulled up and a girl got out of the passenger's seat. She was wearing a sort of fairy costume, a glitter-studded mask strapped across her eyes. She brandished a wand over me, thrust a flyer into my hand and stuck a few more under the wipers of parked cars and took off.

Halloween Ball
Afro-Kilcody Superstores
Adm €5

I stuffed the naggin in my coat pocket and set off towards Barracks Street. The air was thick with coal slack smoke, the odd firework going off with a sound like stitches ripping. Music boomed from the Superstores and jack-o'-lanterns flickered in the windows, candles guttering behind their gap-toothed grins. The front door was open, people spilling onto the step. The bouncer on the door was wearing a Frankenstein costume. I stepped past him and paid a girl sitting on a keg, a biscuit tin full of change on her lap.

Figures milled about in fancy dress, pirates and ghouls and vampires. The walls were draped in bats and bones, the ceiling hung with fake cobwebs. A sluggish beat throbbed from a sound system set up on a raised platform of pallets. Sub-bass and smoky vocals. The DJ was dressed in a Day-Glo one-piece skeleton suit, working the faders on a mixing desk. Some guy in a white coat squeezed by me, stethoscope swinging around his neck.

'Hey,' he yelled into my ear. 'The homeless look. Original.'

I pushed my way through the packed room.

A girl threw her arms around my neck and kissed my cheek. She was poured into shiny black PVC pants and wearing a cat mask that covered her eyes.

'Finnerty!' she shouted over the music.

'Have we met?' I said.

She blinked. Her breath was industrial.

'Sorry. Thought you were someone else.'

Tucked under her arm was a whip.

I squeezed sideways through bodies squashed rush-hour tight. The room blurred with harlequin faces and beatific smiles. Everything had that mellow faraway look. Projected high on the back wall was an old black-and-white 1950s monster film. Huddled in a corner, a guy in a full-face Reaganstein mask snorted a rail of powder off the back of his hand. He pinched at his rubber nostrils and rubbed the surplus powder on his gums.

I gulped whiskey, exhilarated by the strangeness of it all, and found an empty fruit crate and turned it on its side. Someone handed me the biggest, fattest blunt I'd ever seen. I sucked deep, the sweet smoke burning in my lungs. My head grew heavy and lolled like an infant's. I took another drag and rested the back of my skull against the wall and closed my eyes. Someone removed the blunt from my fingers. I groped for the naggin and took a slug and swam inside the deep, bass-heavy throb of the music.

'Hey. Sleeping beauty.'

A young black man was crouched before me, short and slim, with delicate features and huge almond eyes. The party had thinned out and the music was chilled and spacey, the beats slower.

'Looked like you were having a nice dream.' The young man smiled. He had on tailored trousers and pointy-toed boots with Cuban heels, a packet of cigarettes stuffed into the sleeve of a skinny-fit white T-shirt. His arms were whipcord wiry. 'You all right?'

My head reeled a little, a weird field of insulation around my skin, but I was OK, no spinnies, no nausea. The naggin was gone.

'Somebody stole my whiskey,' I said.

The young man jerked his head.

'Come into the back room. You look like you could use some air.'

Groggy and uncoordinated, I followed him into the part of the shop that used to be the hair salon, stepping over empty bottles and beer cans and paper plates blackened with stubbed-out butts.

The back room was empty but for a few chairs and a table strewn with cards. There was a mini-bar fridge in the corner. The young man took two cans of lager from it, pulled the ringtabs and handed me one.

'Sit,' he said. 'It's cool: I work here. What's your name?'

I collapsed into one of the chairs and told him. The beer can was blissfully cold. I rolled it across my cheeks and forehead.

'I'm Jude,' he said, and took the opposite chair.

I spluttered a bit.

'Udechukwu?'

He pulled a face.

'You read the paper.'

I wiped beer from my chin.

'I thought you'd disappeared.'

He pursed his lips.

'What else did you hear?'

'Nothing. It was probably bullshit.'

'Tell me anyway.'

'I heard Gunter Prunty attacked you. Something to do with his girlfriend.'

Jude lit a cigarette.

'I knew Maggie,' he said. 'Nothing happened. I don't go with girls.'

He raised an immaculate eyebrow, picked up the cards and began to shuffle them.

'She got me into a lot of trouble. But I couldn't stay mad at her. My mistake was going to the Guards. I got my boss into trouble. He had to let me go.'

He began to lay the cards out on the table.

It was a Tarot deck, illustrated with Day of the Dead designs, skeletons and flowers. I nodded at the cards.

'It said in the paper you were wrapped up in some sort of voodoo stuff.'

He pulled a face.

'They made that up.'

'Who?'

'Gunter and his friend, the Guard. They told the reporter what to write. It was a cover-up.'

'You're joking.'

He grinned, showing freshly capped teeth.

'I wish.' His voice was melodious, almost sing-song.

'That doesn't make sense,' I said. 'Why would he do that for Gunter?'

Udechukwu shrugged.

'Smokescreen.'

And it was then I realised that the stories Jamey had written were truer than the ones printed in the paper. It was Canavan that Maggie was seeing on the sly, of course. She had lied, and Canavan had gone along with her lie. Udechukwu read my thoughts.

'People don't care if a story is real or not,' he said. 'All that matters is if they believe it.'

He scrutinised the cards, looking rueful.

'Have you ever heard the story of the fool and the skull?' he said.

I shook my head and gulped from the can. It was way late.

'Don't think so.'

He reshuffled the cards.

'A young man was walking a path through the desert. He found a skull and poked it with his staff and said, 'Foolishness killed thee.' The skull replied, 'Foolishness killed me, but I will kill thee.' The young man returned home and told the old men of the village what happened, but they didn't believe him. They'd passed that skull many times but never heard it speak. So the young man said, 'We'll go back to the place of the skull and I'll strike it with my staff, and if it doesn't speak, you can cut off my head.'

'So they retraced his steps to the skull, and a crowd followed them. The young man struck the skull with his staff and said to it, 'Foolishness killed thee', but the skull didn't answer, so he struck it a second time, and still no answer. The crowd grew angry and accused the young man of telling lies and they fell upon him and cut off his head. But then the skull spoke. It said, 'Foolishness killed me, but I killed thee.' '

Udechukwu went back to his cards. I got to my feet and made my way through the debris. There were maybe a dozen stragglers sitting around, bright eyed and red lipped and pale from drinking. I pushed the front door open. The new day was breaking, the sky a gorgeous scarlet, the kind of sky that could break your heart.

~

By December my mother was confined to her sickbed, still wouldn't eat anything more substantial than soup. Most evenings I sat at her bedside and read from one of her Westerns, a yarn about some salty old shooter name of McLean who embarks on one last sojourn across the border to retrieve his trusty horse, Horatio, from the bunch of no-good Mexican bandits who'd rustled him from the livery while McLean was sleeping off a bender in the local cathouse. The story ended with the shooter, having plugged every last bandit and rescued Horatio, bleeding buckets from a gut-shot wound as he sat atop the stoic old horse, who wouldn't rest until he'd ferried his dying master back across the border. My mother's eyes sparkled.

All day long and most of the night she slept, and each slow and sickly hour that passed seemed to suck the life from her body until she shrank beneath the sheets. Sometimes her coughing woke the whole house, painful hacking sounds. Each morning I tidied away the crumpled origami shapes of tissues from her bedside dresser and examined the ugly slugs of phlegm for specks of blood, but there were none. Sometimes after she'd drifted off to sleep, I put the books away and told her about the goings-on in school, or things I'd seen or heard in the village on the way home. The sound of the wind and rain outside reminded me of when I was small and she read to me. Now the roles were reversed. The world was completely out of kilter.

The nights grew longer and colder. Every night when she dozed off I talked until I'd grown weary of the sound of my own voice. I told her about the day I first met Jamey in the market square, and about the trick Jamey and Ollie played on me when I visited their house. I told her about the night Jamey and me went to the Rugby Club. I told her what really happened in the chapel, and about the morning Guard Canavan took me to the Barracks in Ballo. I described what I saw on the camcorder tape. I even told her about the day I hitched to Ballo (leaving out the bit about Miss Ross) and what happened at the old slaughterhouse. And one night I told her that when Jamey walked away, it felt as though something inside me died, like I was a twin whose body had absorbed that of its brother, and now he lived in me. I looked off into space as I spoke, and I didn't see that her eyes had opened until I felt her cold fingers close around my wrist.

'Labhra Loingseach's got donkey's ears,' she whispered.

Christmas was a dismal affair. I gave Mrs Nagle a box of chocolates, which she grunted at and spirited away to the fridge. She was too mean to buy a turkey and would've burned it anyway, so we spent dinner glowering at each other over a miserable little chicken and a plate of soapy spuds and sprouts boiled to mush. I brought a plate up to my mother, but she wouldn't so much as look at it. I couldn't blame her.

New Year's Eve ushered in another year on earth. I lay awake until midnight when the radio squawked Auld Lang Syne. It sounded like a bitter joke. Sometimes when my mother woke, she had trouble remembering who or where she was. Dr Orpen couldn't help. Eat, he said. Rest. Cut down on the fags. Any time I tried to discuss money, he said we'd settle our account at a later date.

One day when he called to check on what he called her 'progress', he glanced at Mrs Nagle, who was scrubbing out a burnt pot in the sink, head cocked, earwigging as usual. He put his arm around my shoulder and took me outside.

'You and Phyllis have been doing Trojan work,' he said, squinting against the light. 'But at this stage I think your mother would be better off in St Luke's.'

'The home?'

He fixed me with clear blue eyes.

'This house is perishing, son. She stays here the rest of the winter, she'll get her death.'

He glanced at his wristwatch. I visualised a pendulum being set in motion.

'I'll make all the arrangements,' he said. 'Call me in the morning.'

I watched him walk down the path and into the cold, bright afternoon, his shadow scissoring the hard ground, then I went inside and repeated what he'd said.

'Nonsense,' Mrs Nagle scoffed. 'We're doing our level best here, John. I'm sure your mother would much rather be in her own house than some old knacker yard of a home.'

I desperately wanted to believe her.

That night as I was trying to get to sleep, I heard the landing creak and saw Mrs Nagle standing in my bedroom doorway, grey hair slithering down her shoulders. She stood for what seemed like a very long time, just watching, before she turned away and softly closed my door. I was disquieted by her uncharacteristic stillness, as though the daytime Mrs Nagle, the thick-necked here's-me-head-me-arse-is-coming Mrs Nagle, was some kind of act, a front for an even colder, steelier creature. My mother was getting feebler, and here was this old hatchet growing taller and stronger with every passing day, like there was some queer transfusion of energies taking place.

I turned on my side and tried to sleep, struck by a terrible feeling of being displaced, homesick, even though I was home. I kept trying to imagine what life would be like without my mother, and my chest ached.

Some time later I awoke with a jolt. The night was very still, disturbed only by the sound of branches fingering the slates and the bones of the old house groaning. I got out of bed and went to check on my mother.

Her bed was empty, the covers thrown back. For a moment I thought perhaps her sickness had lifted and her senses had returned and maybe she was downstairs making breakfast or reading the paper, but there was no one in the kitchen except for Mrs Nagle, dozing beside the crumbling embers of the fire. I pulled my boots on and threw a coat over my thermals and checked the backyard and the surrounding fields.

Everywhere was white, so white it almost hurt to look at. Icicles hung from the gates and the grass was covered in what looked like pale moondust. Frost had petrified the nettles and the puddles on the ground were cracked panes of glass. I called out for my mother, and the chill turned my breath to plumes of white.

The sky in the east began to brighten as I searched around our house as far as Lambert's land. I hurried across the frozen fields, scanning the landscape for my mother's form, kept going until the ground deteriorated into marsh. Rabbit droppings pebbled the clumps of grass. Ferns curled from the ground, delicate spiderwebs strung from dock-leaf fronds, briars and brambles intertwined in weirdly pornographic tableaux. The edge of Lambert's shallow pond was jellied with frogspawn, dead tadpoles preserved in cryogenic ice.

The ground grew spongy and uncertain beneath my boots, threatening to suck me under, and I imagined creatures writhing below the subsoil, hideous squids with saucer eyes and birds' beaks and sucker-studded tentacles. Panic began to rise in my chest. I was lost. My mother was lost.

Daybreak spread across the earth, bleak

light that promised neither warmth nor hope, merely its own inevitable self. Then I saw her, still and bewildered amidst the gorse bushes. She was wearing only her nightdress, violently shivering.

'Ma,' I called out. 'You'll get your death.'

She turned and stared at me, eyes urgent, teeth clicking.

'I have to c-collect the children's allowance.'

I took off my coat and wrapped it around her shoulders and helped her home through the merciless winter dawn. I put her to bed and then hurried into the bathroom to run her a hot bath.

Mrs Nagle was bent over the sink — she still hadn't gotten into the habit of locking the door. At first I thought she was washing her hands. She murmured in a low voice, like a chant. Her right hand was held palm down over a bowl of milk. A length of twine dangled from her wrist, knotted at intervals like a rosary. She'd placed a lit candle on the soap dish. The draught from the open door made its flame flicker. She glanced up at the mirror, saw my face and whirled around.

'You put the heart across me,' she said, leaning her back against the rim of the sink, blocking my view. She was wearing one of my mother's dresses, but it didn't fit; the sleeves came down to her elbows and the hem stopped above her knees.

'What are you doing?' I said.

'Nothing. Go back to bed. You're still half asleep. You must have been dreaming.'

Old Crow knows his lives have been no more than dream stories the soul tells itself at the second of death, that delicious alchemical rush as transfiguration occurs and the whatever-it-is essence converts into black light, kinetic heat, and you tilt your wings and slip and shape-shift through to the somewhere-else, transcending absolute black in a death-defying virtuoso act, and all the assembled souls in the halls of eternity go Wow! and Bravo! and Who Is That Daring Flying Machine? and applaud the sight of animate matter transmuted into streams of electrons and — weeeee! — streaking through power lines and telex systems, a strobe of dark lightning slashing the fabric of the sky, senses laser sharp, eyes like Zeiss lenses set to turbo-zoom, its body's rhythms and mind's melodies transposed into the thrilling drone of power pylons, the stuff of thermonuclear dreams, an electric ghost whose presence can be divined sometimes by the living, manifest as background radiation in their cell memories, insinuated into their analogues, an inkling, slightly acrid, a sudden pressure drop as its form flits through the white mist of television interference, just about glimpsed when a heavy fall of rain splits the screen into component pixels, its presence faintly sensed as the living dead slouch in their sweats in front of the box, biorhythms at lowest ebb, a hair's breadth from death, the last metabolic stop before terminus est, the white-noised no-man's-land where the dead and the living dead intermingle and become one.

10

To enter St Luke's Hospital, you passed through a trellis embroidered with creepers and hydrangeas that gave onto a modest little garden bisected by a paved path, benches placed around the grass verge, grey blocks of buildings looming on three sides. Inside the main dining room the radio piped incongruously chirpy pop music. A television sat on a shelf bolted to the wall about ten feet off the floor, the sound turned down, Doris Day flouncing around in her pyjamas. Bath chairs and wheelchairs were stacked and folded in corners. The floor smelled scrubbed and carbolic.

The residents were mostly perplexed-looking women, all elbows and angles, like wooden dolls propped awkwardly in their chairs. Some clutched soft toys in hands that were mostly knuckle, and muttered to their shoes when they weren't casting furtive glances at the pastel-painted walls.

Some were scrawny and spindly, others double-chinned and flabby, their arms and legs as soft muscled as those of infants. A spindly stick-figured woman with bifocals padded around in repetitive paths, her slippers describing complex bee patterns, a security anklet periodically activating the front-door lock with a loud click.

In the couple of weeks she'd been there, my mother had lost even more weight and seemed to retreat to the back of her mind. Her speech became hard to decipher, and what I could make out was vague and befuddled. The nurses tut-tutted to each other about her bloods being like water and speculating as to whether or not she needed to be put on a drip. She spent most of her time strapped into a chair like a toddler at a restaurant, a cup of mush in her trembling hand, eyes dull and glazed.

On the days it wasn't raining the nurses encouraged me to take her out into the garden. I helped her into a coat and guided her down the narrow corridor, baby steps, stopping every so often as her body was racked with shuddering fits, and the birdwoman with the glasses bumped against our backs like some malfunctioning automaton as we shuffled in slow motion towards the door. One of the nurses came out to poke a code into the keypad on the wall, and when the buzzer sounded she shoved the door and held it open until we were outside.

We'd sit on a bench and watch small birds settle on the trellis. I'd light my mother's cigarettes and take them from her fingers when they'd burned down to the butt, blathering about the weather, uncomfortably aware that she'd be vexed with me for speaking to her like she was a slow child. Truth was, I didn't know how to act. I was acutely aware of the nurses watching me, like they were gauging my performance as a son.

Sometimes as I was leaving, my mother would try to manoeuvre herself onto the nurse's blind side and slip out the door. 'C'mon,' she'd mutter, 'we'll go home,' the careful enunciation of each word seeming to require all her energy and concentration. For a moment I'd indulge the fantasy of the two of us sneaking off and maybe stealing a car and holding up petrol stations and living out the rest of our lives as fugitives from the law. But instead I took her gently by the arm and parked her at the nurse's station.

'I can't bring you with me,' I'd say, feeling like she must have felt when she left me in the classroom on my first day of school. And I'd force myself to walk away, aware of her clear, watery eyes staring after me, burning through my back, my ribcage, right into my rotten little heart.

All I wanted to do after those visits was go out and get drunk, to feel numbed from what was happening. One evening I stopped by Hyland's off-licence instead of going home. The old man was in the back room watching the soaps as usual. I eased the door open a crack, just enough for me to squeeze through, not enough to rattle the bell, and grabbed a six-pack of beer from the fridge and stuck it under my coat. I crept out and hurried across the square to the cemetery and prised the lid off a bottle using the edge of a headstone.

Soon it began to batter down with sleet, one of those vicious, vindictive squalls that make your ears and teeth ache. I stuffed the remaining bottles into my coat. Weighed down and clinking, I ducked into Donahue's and ordered a glass and brought it out into the empty beer garden where I could top it up without getting caught. The big gas heater made my face feel sunburned. Sleet battered the perspex canopy overhead.

Shortly before closing time a girl came out nursing her vodka-and-something. She was alone, and I couldn't help but stare. You could tell she'd been very pretty, maybe even beautiful, when she was younger. The bone structure was still intact, but a patchwork of smile lines had frozen in place around her huge, starved eyes. She had on a pair of low-riding jeans and a top embroidered with flower patterns. Something about her in that blouse was more affecting than if she'd dressed her age, as if the wish to stay young was enough to carry it off. She shivered from the cold, fumbled with her lighter and cigarettes and caught my eye.

'Have you seen Gunter Prunty around?' she said, hugging herself. She spoke with a London-Irish accent. 'Big chap.'

I shook my head.

'Good.'

She sat beside me on the bench. I guessed she was more than a little drunk.

'How do you know Gunter?' I said.

'I'm his lover.'

She let the end of the word uncurl off her tongue like some kind of party trick, and took a gulp of vodka.

'My name's Maggie.'

She offered me her hand. I took it, careful not to squeeze too hard, and told her my name.

'Well, John,' she said. 'You'll never get a woman with that handshake.'

I didn't know what to say, so I just let go of her fingers and sipped beer.

'You used to knock about with Jamey Corboy,' she said. 'He was fun.'

She set the tumbler down and nodded at my glass.

'Want another?'

Before I could reply, she looked around and caught the eye of a young lad clearing tables and ordered us more drinks. When she opened her bag to pay, you could see it was a mess in there, money and make-up and receipts. She gave the boy a tenner and told him to keep the change.

'Cheers,' she said, and clinked her glass off mine. We sat in silence for a while and then she said: 'I bought you a drink. The least you can do is make idle conversation.'

'Why don't you talk and I'll join in when you get going,' I said.

'Jesus. A listener.' She rolled her eyes. 'How rare. What if I tell you about the time I was abused by my brother-in-law.'

I didn't expect that.

'What age were you?'

'Twenty-four.'

'Twenty-*four*. That's not abuse.'

'Isn't it?'

She fiddled with a ragged friendship bracelet tied around her wrist.

'Ask me something else,' she said.

'Any kids?'

'Two abortions. You?'

It went on like that for some time. I told her she had the biggest eyes I'd ever seen on a girl. She said boys like me always fall for the Bambi routine, before they realise girls like her are more trouble than they're worth.

'Y'know,' she said, 'I used to see you every morning on your way to school. You looked so cute in your uniform.'

I reddened.

'I never saw you,' I said.

She lit another cigarette.

'Maybe I should've worn a shorter skirt. Then you might have noticed. What age are you anyway?'

'Nineteen.'

She ignored the lie, or let herself believe it, and knocked back most of her drink.

The more we talked the closer she sat to me. I can't remember which of us made the move, or if we both did at the same time, but sitting there in that empty yard among the kegs and the benches, we kissed. Funny how people who don't even know each other can kiss like that, like it means something. All the time, warning bells were going off in my head about what would happen if someone saw us and it got back to Gunter, but that only seemed to make it better.

When the staff threw us out I walked her to her flat.

'Nightcap?' she said. 'Gunter's on the late shift.'

In that moment I could see how it all played out. We'd go inside and sit at her kitchen table and have just the one, and just the one would become another one, and we'd move to the sofa, both knowing what was going to happen, we wouldn't be able to stop it; she'd lead me into the bedroom, both of us too numb to feel bad, there'd be no guilt, it'd feel like we were forgiven no matter what we did, and when she woke I'd be gone and she wouldn't care either way. It was like the deed was already done somehow, and to make it real would have been just a formality, repeating with our bodies what we'd already pictured in our minds.

'No thanks,' I said.

'You sure?'

Those huge eyes. I thought about Gunter, and what he'd done to me and Jamey. And then I thought about Guard Canavan and how he forced me to rat Jamey out.

'No, I'm not sure. But I'd better go home. I have to be up early.'

'Work?'

'I have to visit my mother. She's in a home.'

Maggie guffawed but then stopped herself just as suddenly.

'Sorry,' she said. 'I don't know why I did that.'

When I woke my eyes were filled with water and my hands clawed at the sheets. There was a yellow stream of dried sick on my pillow. My mouth tasted vile. I stripped the bed and shambled downstairs, brought up short by the sight of an envelope on the doormat. Jamey's handwriting. I dumped the soiled bedclothes on the floor and tore it open. There was a postcard inside, paperclipped to a few sheets of paper. The picture on the front showed a trio of musicians sitting on a patterned carpet playing exotic-looking flutes and hand drums. The caption read: *The Master Musicians of Joujouka*. On the back was a single sentence, printed in block capitals.

I AM ONLY ESCAPED TO TELL THEE.

I sat at the kitchen table and leafed through the papers.

The Ghost in the Machine
by Jamey Corboy

The connecting flight from Barcelona to Boukhalef was delayed by fog. Three hours spent loitering sore-eyed and adenoidal in a harshly lit terminal before boarding. It was a short hop, which was some solace, and when they touched down he shuffled through the giant vacuum hose of the deplaning tunnel onto the travelator, down two flights of steps to join the queue for customs check, freeze-dried by the chilly airplane air.

The guy from the car service was slumped into a chair in the arrivals lounge, wearily holding a sign bearing his name — Mr Fixer.

'I was about to pitch a tent,' the driver said as the terminal doors slid apart, admitting a hairdryer blast of wet heat. 'Wanna put your case in the trunk?'

'No thanks.'

They walked towards the short-term parking lot. Fixer felt microwaved back to life. Already his skin prickled with sweat.

'Australian?' he said to the driver.

'Kiwi.'

'Sorry.'

'No worries.'

Evening traffic swarmed through the medina. The light was unreal. He took out his wallet and checked the thin wad of dirhams he'd bought at the currency-exchange counter, hoping it wasn't one of those hotels that demanded a credit-card number or deposit on arrival in case you needed to use the phone or the mini-bar. He didn't mind the travelling so much, but the incidentals ate into his profit margin. A few cent lost on the exchange rate here, a cup of coffee or a newspaper there. It all added up, receipts replacing the notes in his wallet. Expenses will be covered, the client assured him. Well, it was their dollar. He could just as easily have done the job in his lab. They could have Fed-Exed the DAT, could have emailed the file, but no, too cautious. Too paranoid.

The driver dropped him off at the hotel. He checked in and went straight to his room. The lights of his room flickered on and the air-conditioning hummed into life as he stuck his key card into the wall slot. All hotel rooms are the same, he thought. You only pay for the size of the foyer.

He went to the window and gazed out on the harbour. Evening was falling. If not for the grey haze, he might have seen right across the Strait of Gibraltar. Fatigue conjured phantom shapes in the mist.

He placed the suitcase on the floor and took his shoes off and lay down on the bed. Sleep crawled over him, tendrils of mist seeping through the a/c grille, inseminating his dreams with wailing voices like calls to prayer, echoes of past exorcisms. And he fell, as he always did, pushed from a plane or the top of a twenty-storey building, only to jolt awake as if zapped with defibrillator paddles moments before hitting the pavement.

He stared at the ceiling and waited for some integral part of himself to disentangle from the dream stuff and re-enter his body. It was way too early. His body clock was all over the place. He sat in a chair by the window and waited for the sun to rise. In time, the fog lifted just enough for him to see ships in dock. Ports are portals, he told himself. Just like home.

He went through the list of contact numbers in his phone and dialled the airline.

'Hello,' he said. 'I'd like to change my return flight.'

'Certainly, sir. Can I have your details?'

He took his ticket and boarding pass from his inside pocket and called out numbers.

The American appeared in the lobby at ten thirty. Tall, dressed in a T-shirt and khakis, lantern jawed, beard the same length as his cropped hair.

'Flight OK?'

'Fine. Is it far?'

'We can walk it from here.'

They left the hotel and zigzagged through

the market stalls set up in the souk: cobblers, leatherworkers, coppersmiths, fruit vendors, rugs and throws.

'Sorry they dragged you out here,' the American said. 'Management wouldn't authorise release of the tapes. You know how it is. Piracy.'

'Big money, huh?'

'No kidding. Priority release. First single off the album.'

The American explained the urgency of the situation. The track had to be fixed, mastered and remixed for a radio edit within the week. Then there was artwork, manufacturing, release-schedule deadlines, the press campaign.

The American was a producer of some description. Fixer had done a quick internet search and turned up his name on a couple of big records. The American had been in exile here for years, knew all the Berber and Chaabi musicians. A contact in New York had commissioned field recordings; exotic flavour for some big-league act. He'd recorded about half an hour of music, earmarked a twenty-second sample, but when it was inserted into the main track, there was some sort of technical anomaly. A spanner in the works. He put the distress call out three days ago.

They ducked into a narrow alley and came to a decrepit building next door to a barber's shop. It looked like a nuclear bunker. The American took out his keys, unlocked a padlock, slid the door across. They went up a spiral staircase into a cluttered room dimmed with blinds, the air tangible with the faintly cooked smell of kef. Electrical leads coiled like snakes on patterned rugs. Bullet mics and pop shields. A mixing desk that looked like something from the early days of the space programme.

'I'll play you the tapes,' the American said. He sat in a swivel chair before a computer monitor, tapped the keys, wheeled over to the mixing desk and shoved up the master fader.

Beats pounded from powerful speakers. After a couple of minutes the main track peeled apart to reveal a passage of skreeling, ear-splitting sounds, like chanters or bag-pipes.

'What's the problem?' Fixer said.

The American stood, palms splayed on the padded lip of the console.

'This.'

He prodded a series of buttons, silencing elements of the track until he'd isolated the anomaly. A wailing sound, like wind. No matter how many times Fixer heard it, it chilled him. Each specimen differed subtly, a minor variation on the last, as though the sound were a mutating virus, migrating through phantom frequencies, broadcasting from the ether. Fixer imagined he could hear traces of the fog in the sound, troubling the AI dreams of the digital hardware as it had troubled his own.

'I don't know where it's coming from,' the American said. 'I've tried everything. Duplicated, remixed, bounced tracks all over the place . . . I went through every channel, but I can't isolate it. It's like it doesn't exist until several tracks are playing in concert.'

'OK. I've heard enough.'

'Can you get rid of it?'

'Of course.'

Fixer cracked open his briefcase and removed the apparatus. Two ancient analogue tape machines labelled A and B, twinned by an umbilical cord of connecting jack. Clunky switches, inputs on the side, decibel meters set into the casing.

'Wow,' the American said. 'Old school.'

'You've no idea.' Fixer depressed the record switches on both machines. 'Hook these up to the desk and play it again.'

The American did as he was told and cued the track. This time the monitor screen showed jagged sine waves, but no sound came from the speakers.

'Fuck,' said the American, and began to fiddle with the faders. 'Where's it gone?'

'In here.' Fixer tapped the tape machines. 'I'll explain in a minute. Just let it play.'

When the track finished, he clicked the stop button on each recorder and unplugged the connecting jack.

'Now,' he said. 'I've transferred your master track and stored it in the unit labelled A. It's clean. The infected frequencies have been quarantined in B. We call it ghost washing. To reinstate the master, set the desk to record and simply press the play button on unit A. It'll only take the length of the song. But keep the main-desk fader down unless you want room sounds corrupting your track.'

The American stared at the ancient tape machine.

'This is state of the art production,' he said, 'and you want me to take a feed from that thing?'

'Relax. The integrity of the recording has been preserved.'

'How?'

'It just has. Trust me, I do this for a living.'

The American looked doubtful.

'What about the other one? The one containing the weird noises?'

'It'll need to be disposed of. I'll take care of it.'

'That's it?'

'That's it.'

Fixer placed the B unit in his briefcase and snapped it shut.

'Just remember, keep the volume all the way down when you're reinstalling the track to the desk. I'll be at the hotel if you need me. You can return the other unit when you're finished.'

He descended the spiral staircase and let himself out and was soon lost in the commotion of the market place. He stuck his hand out and hailed a cab.

'Boukhalef, please,' he told the driver.

When they reached the airport, Fixer paid the cabbie and checked in at the self-service terminal, then proceeded directly to the departure gate. He browsed through a couple of stalls and bought a cup of coffee from a vending machine. Half an hour prior to boarding, he stepped into the men's room, found an empty cubicle and shut the door. He dialled the studio. The American answered. He sounded anxious.

'Listen,' he said. 'Your black-box recorder. You took the wrong one or something. When I transferred the track back to the desk, all I got was those weird noises. I called by your hotel, but you weren't picking up.'

'That's because I'm not there. Do you have a pen?'

'Why?'

'Just write this down.'

He called out the details. Had to raise his voice in order to be heard over an announcement on the airport PA.

'Now,' he said. 'If you instruct your client to deposit ten thousand dollars in that account by five o'clock this afternoon your time, you'll receive a package containing the unit with the clean track in a couple of days. Input as instructed. If the money doesn't go through to the account this afternoon, I erase the track. Do you understand?'

He hung up the phone and went to the bar at the end of the departures lounge. Ordered a dry Martini and sipped it, looking out the great slanted windows.

'You've got the right idea,' the barman said. He sounded French.

'Excuse me?'

'Looks like you'll be here a while. All flights are grounded.'

He gestured through the windows. A yellow haze had descended on the runway.

'Fog.'

With my mother in the hospital, Mrs Nagle could no longer justify staying in the house.

She knew it too, and made a point of keeping out of my way. The daily visits to St Luke's kept me preoccupied, but the tension in the house soon grew so palpable it was like a headache.

'Mrs Nagle,' I said one morning, standing with my back to the fire, 'I don't know what I would've done without you this past while.'

'Ah,' she said, getting her teeth into a walnut whirl, 'think nothing of it. I couldn't see you stuck.'

I cleared my throat.

'I'd say you must miss your own house though.'

She gnawed the chocolate coating off the walnut like a horse at a sugar lump.

'Faith, I do not,' she said. 'That kip is cold as the hob of hell. The landlord won't do a thing about it. Doesn't give a hoot if an old woman catches her death.'

I picked up the poker and gave the fire a stir.

'Still and all though, you'd want to keep an eye on the place. It might get broken into if people think it's empty.'

She tossed her head in the air.

'Sure there's nothing of mine worth taking.'

I tapped soot off the poker.

'Thing is, Mrs Nagle, what with my mother

in St Luke's and all, I can take care of things now. Your work here is done, as they say.'

'Indeed and it's not,' she said. 'Don't you need looking after?'

'Oh, I'll be fine. I'm a big boy.'

She plucked up another chocolate and perched the box on the arm of my mother's chair.

'And what are you going to live on? You've no skill nor trade, nor no head for money. Just like your mother. She was a hard worker, but she wasn't a wealthy woman.'

Her use of the past tense riled me almost as much as the insincere look of sympathy she affected. She banished that look with the rest of the walnut whirl and approximated something like concern.

'All the more reason for me to keep an eye on you. We're rubbing along just fine, aren't we? Anyway — ' She faked a cough. ' — I've given the landlord my notice. I allowed with the money I save on rent I can spoil you rotten. A young man needs a good woman to look after him. And your mother's in no fit state — '

'Don't you say another word about my mother.'

She put a half-eaten walnut whirl back in the box and stood, hands on her big broad hips.

'It's time you faced up to it, son. She's not long for this world. I'm the only family you have now.'

My stomach churned.

'You're not my family, Mrs Nagle. You'll have to leave. I've tried asking you nicely, but you won't listen.'

She took a step back and drew herself up to her full height. I thought her head might bump off the ceiling.

'John Devine,' she said. 'How could you do this to me? Your mother would be ashamed. You're like my own son.'

She grabbed her coat from the back of a kitchen chair.

'You need to cool off, me bucko,' she said. 'I'm going out for a minute, and when I get back I'll make us a nice lunch and we'll forget all about this little tiff.'

She swept out the door, head high.

I put the poker down and slumped in the armchair.

I went through my pockets and found Har Farrell's business card and stepped into the hall and dialled the number scrawled on the back. He answered on the second ring.

'Young John,' he said. 'What way are you?'

It sounded like there were rashers frying in the circuitry of his phone. I told him about my mother having fallen sick, but he'd already heard, so I updated him on everything that had happened since Mrs Nagle moved in.

'That conniving old bag,' he growled. 'How can I help?'

'I need to change the locks.'

He grunted.

'Easy done. But we'll need to get her out of the house for an hour or so. Isn't she a holy roller?'

'She goes to evening Mass every weekday.'

'Good enough. Next time she leaves, ring. I'll be ready.'

I could almost hear his cheeks click from grinning.

'I've been waiting a long time to get my own back on that old bag. *Athníonn ciaróg, ciaróg eile.*'

'Come again?'

'One earwig recognises another.'

When I arrived at St Luke's that day, the nurse made her usual comment about how my mother was lucky to have such a good son who visited so often. I couldn't bring myself to tell her that I had nowhere else to go, that a bossy old woman had taken over my home.

It was a fresh day, cold but bright, so I took

my mother out into the garden. There was no one around. The possibility of breaking her out of that place, even for a little while, suddenly seemed very real. There was nothing to detain us.

I put my arm around my mother's shoulder and guided her through the trellis and down the drive. It seemed absurdly easy. To either side of us, psychedelic flowerbeds glowed, daffodils and bluebells all nodding their approval.

The front gate came closer with every step. I grew impatient with how long we were taking, so I placed my mother's hands around my neck and stooped and lifted her onto my back. She was no weight, and I was soon able to put a good distance between us and the hospital, my hands locked under her haunches, running as swiftly as possible, fast enough to spirit her away before she crumbled to her shinbones. As we approached the centre of the village I heard a sound so familiar it could've been coming from inside my head, a sound I wouldn't have believed was real only I felt my mother's breath in my ear.

She was giggling.

People gawked as we crossed the market square. I set my mother down on the shelf of the Father Carthy monument. A sour-looking woman in a housecoat marched up to me and said, 'That woman shouldn't be out of doors.'

'Mind your own business,' I said.

She huffed off, throwing suspicious looks over her shoulder. I glared in her wake, indignant and a little bit ashamed. Even though it was a mild afternoon, my mother was shivering. I rubbed her hands and tried to get her circulation going. We needed to be indoors, away from the prying eyes of busybodies who might recognise us and ring the hospital. Somewhere safe and warm.

Down Barracks Street and into Donahue's. It was a Saturday and the place was full of people watching the match, but the snug was free and nobody bothered with us. I ordered two hot whiskeys and wiped the dribble from my mother's chin with my sleeve and peered into her glassy eyes, tried to see beyond the veil of her glazed stare. The image came to mind of a child trapped under the surface of a frozen lake, clawing at the underside, a submerged shape bumping against the ice.

I stood, undecided about whether to buy another drink or make ready to leave, when I saw Gunter Prunty looming in the doorway. I shrank back into the shadows but it was too late: he'd spotted us. He made a beeline for our table, big barrel chest bulging under an AC/DC T-shirt with the sleeves cut off. He had a sleeve-length tattoo on each arm, some sort of Celtic symbol that snaked and spiralled all the way from his shoulders to his elbows.

I met his eyes and steeled myself for trouble. Gunter stared, unmoving, as if stumped for words.

My mother's hand went out to her drink, but she misjudged and knocked it off the table. The glass bounced off the tiles, splashing whiskey, and rolled between Gunter's motorcycle boots. He stared at the glass a moment, then crouched and picked it up and placed it on the table. He strode over to the bar and put his foot up on the rail, beckoned to one of the girls serving and jerked his thumb in our direction. The girl nodded. I wasn't sure what was going on. Maybe he was trying to have us thrown out. I couldn't decide whether to stay put or get my mother out of there, but then the bargirl came over carrying two more whiskeys on a tray.

'That gentleman at the bar paid for these,' she said and pointed at Gunter, who was getting stuck into a pint of stout.

It was the first time I'd ever heard him called a gentleman. He took his glass and went out the back for a smoke. My mother watched him go. We sipped our whiskeys, but my mother seemed to lose interest after a couple of slurps, so I helped her to her feet and took her outside and hefted her onto my back. I started to walk, didn't know where, but we had to keep moving.

My feet led me straight across the square and through the chapel gates and under the arch. I dipped my hand in the holy water font and blessed myself and daubed a bit on my mother's brow and led her to a pew. We had the whole chapel to ourselves. The solemn atmosphere and dim light were calm and comforting. Beams of light slanted diagonally through the stained-glass windows and pooled on the floor, the colour of oil in water.

After a few moments my mother's chin dipped to her chest and she began to softly snore. I let her doze and listened to the faint dripping sounds and echoes of shuffling footsteps as the occasional pensioner wandered in to pray or light a candle.

My eyes took in the stone saints, the fourteen Stations of the Cross, the soft light favouring the tabernacle, the statue of the crucified Christ, His face turned away as if in disgust. We were on our own. Nobody was watching over us.

I put my head back until it touched the pew and stared up at the domed chapel roof until I felt dizzy.

The tolling of the Angelus bell brought me back into focus. Soon the priest and the altar boys would be preparing for evening Mass. Mrs Nagle would be getting ready to leave the house, pulling on her woolly hat and coat and spraying herself in sickly sweet perfume.

Outside, the setting sun had turned the whole village honey-coloured. I hoisted my mother onto my shoulders once more and we set off for the hospital, my footsteps slow. The smell of fried onions caught my heart, that Saturday smell from when I was small, my favourite day, when my mother was off work and I'd laze around and read my comics while she cooked us a steak.

Smells flooded the evening, smoke from the chimneys, real smells mingling with imaginary ones drifting from the past, the smell of my mother's perfume as we walked to Mass on Sunday, the smell of incense in the chapel, the no-smell-at-all of Jamey's house, the smell of Ollie's apple drops, the fried eggs my mother made me and Jamey, the white-scared smell of sweat in Ballo Garda Station, the smell of strawberry juice on my hands all summer, the reek of the rubbish dump, the smell of Molly Ross's body as she straddled me, the flyspray smell of Mrs Nagle, the smell of Jude Udechukwu's cologne, the smell of Maggie's breath against my skin, the smell of the creepers and flowers hanging from the trellis at St Luke's, the carbolic soap smell as they buzzed us through the door, the nurse's face puce with anger as she took my mother from me and instructed one of the attendants to wrap her in a blanket and put her to bed, and then she took me into her office and gave me a roasting, telling me how my mother could have caught pneumonia or hypothermia and was I trying to kill the woman or what. The next time I came to visit, she warned me, I wouldn't be allowed in unless I wore a security anklet.

I didn't care. They were only doing what they thought was best, stretching out her days the way a miser would count his money. But those days were too precious not to spend. I didn't want her whole life to become diminished by those last days of sickness. The way I saw it, her death couldn't come soon enough, all the better to preserve her memories of everything that happened in her life, even the dreams of what never came to pass.

Mrs Nagle had left for Mass by the time I got home. I checked every room in the house, even the backyard, but there was no sign, so I rang Har Farrell. Within minutes his van pulled up at the gate. He swaggered up the path dressed in a boiler suit, carrying a toolbox.

He grinned through the whiskers he'd grown since the summer, which gave him the appearance of a slightly deranged bear, and set the toolbox on the front step, a big blue monstrosity that opened into stepped shelves and secret compartments like some sort of Chinese puzzle.

'Put the kettle on,' he said. 'Two teabags, three sugars and a tooth full of milk.'

Har worked quickly, drilling and screwdrivering, pausing only to gulp his tea. He replaced the locks and installed a Chubb and fitted dead bolts to the back and front doors. When he was finished he packed up the toolbox and handed me a new set of keys.

'Gather that earwig's belongings and dump them out the front,' he said, climbing back into the van. 'And don't fall for that little-old-lady tripe. If you don't stand up to her now, you'll never be rid. She'll bury the both of us if we're not careful.'

I did as he instructed. Everything Mrs Nagle owned, her girdles and undergarments, her chocolates, I threw them into a rubbish sack deposited on the front lawn. The grass had grown long, the shrubs wild and tangled in the absence of my mother's hands.

I locked the doors and went through the house opening windows, as if to exorcise Mrs Nagle's presence from every room. I emptied the bin and cleaned out the kitchen cupboards. I even emptied out the cubbyhole under the stairs, and found the old crossbow and quiver full of arrows Har had given me for my tenth birthday. They were wrapped in an old coal sack, coated in bits of slack but free of rust. I clawed through the clutter that had accumulated under my mother's armchair, chocolate wrappers and newspapers and dust bunnies. And something else. A book.

I pulled it out.

Harper's Compendium of Bizarre Nature Facts

My mother had kept it all this time. I dusted off the cover and flipped through the pages. The plates and illustrations were like childhood flashbacks. The inscription on the flyleaf read:

To John
Phyllis Nagle

My scalp crawled. The book's pages felt like dead skin in my hands.

I took the book and the crossbow and quiver outside. I placed the book on the front path and touched my lighter to the corners of the pages. A slight breeze fanned the blue and orange flames. Pages withered and blackened into cinders that lifted into the air like moths. I sat on the step with the crossbow cradled across my lap and watched them burn.

'You found your book then.'

Mrs Nagle stood at the front gate, surveying her belongings spilling out of the sack and onto the grass.

I hauled the bowstring back along the bolt groove and cocked it. Then I took an arrow from the quiver and placed it in the breech and stood to face Mrs Nagle.

'Go home,' I said. 'And stay there.'

That night I dozed in the armchair until the sound of raindrops splattering the windows and plonking in the empty fireplace woke me. The drizzle swelled to a monotonous deluge, hissing incessantly against the slates. Once I'd loved to listen to that sound while I snuggled under the covers, safe in the knowledge that the fire was crackling in the grate downstairs and my mother was reading in her armchair, but now the downpour just sounded like deranged voices, the music of madness. Rain, a sound I'd always associated with my mother's headaches, her Sunday afternoon lie-downs. The boredom, sitting alone in an empty house, trying to amuse myself. Now she was gone, but the feeling was the same.

When the rain stopped and the sun came up, I dragged myself upstairs, feeling shivery and disembodied, and I slept right through to the afternoon, when the phone woke me.

It was one of the nurses from St Luke's.

'You'd better come in,' she said. 'Your mother's failing.'

The sky over Kilcody was deep red, big-bellied clouds moving across its expanse like herds of woolly mammoths. I hurried towards the village, powerless to stop what was happening. It was as though all the moments that made up our lives had been set in sequence like dominoes, a succession of trigger events, each precipitating the next, the number of our days preordained and planned since the beginning of time, and we were all no more than creatures made of billions of specks of dust sucked into the collapsing stars of our fates.

I wanted to ask those fatalistic stars for a reprieve, a pardon. Lambs bleated in the fields, the plaintive vibrato of their cries weirdly human, as though they too were appealing for mercy. But there was no going back. I propelled myself forward until I reached St Luke's. The flowerbeds were all in bloom, white blossoms scattered on the grass like snowflakes. A sparrow perched on the trellis. I rang the buzzer and one of the nurses ushered me into a room filled with beds, sleeping women, dried-out husks, heads sunk into pillows, noses up like they were smelling something.

The curtains were three-quarters drawn around my mother's bed, tubes and catheters everywhere. Her chest rose and fell, each breath taking great effort. I sat beside the bed and brushed the hair from my mother's brow and took her scrawny hand. She opened her eyes and managed a wan smile. I gave her a sip from the glass of water on her bedside locker. She tried to speak, but it wasn't her voice, just the ghost of it, as though her own given voice had been sucked out by a succubus and this hoarse whisper was all that was left.

'Remember the mixo hare?' she said. 'When you were small?'

'I remember,' I whispered, afraid that if I raised my voice her body would crumble like ash. She seemed about to say something else, but then her eyelids slowly closed.

Outside, the golden evening light faded to a

washed-out yellow, then twilight, then darkness. I sat by the bed and kept vigil into the early hours, paralysed by the reality of what was happening, her dying, *she's dying*, that thought stuck on repeat, over and over until it became meaningless and I just wanted it all to be done, and then the opposite thought followed on its heels, I wanted my mother to stay with me, those contrary thoughts bound to each other, each chasing the other's tail, looping in circles for hours.

Shortly before dawn broke, she came back into herself. Her eyes were as bright as stars, fixed on an indistinct point, like those of a blind woman. She groped for my hand and asked me the time. I told her, and she seemed satisfied with my answer and fell back asleep. Soon her breathing grew more troubled and her body began to tremble. Something in me recognised those shudders, and I knew she was entering the throes. I called for the nurse. She examined my mother, became brisk and businesslike, and I realised she'd done this many times before.

'I'll go for the priest,' she said. 'I hope there's time. Do you have a cigarette?'

I took the box from my pocket and offered it to her, but she shook her head and opened the window.

'Light one up. The smell might rouse her a

bit. Might give her that last bit of pleasure.'

'Will we get into trouble?'

'Say nothing. Anyone asks, pretend you didn't know any better.'

I sat and breathed smoke over my mother. Her body shivered with movements like labour contractions. I thought of the night she gave birth to me, except now she was birthing herself, out of her life and into her death, and with each inhalation she drew in the smoke and with each exhalation she expelled the last of her breath. Her hand grasped my hand like it must have grasped the midwife's as she pushed me out of her womb, and I urged her towards what lay beyond.

The priest arrived, bleary-eyed and dishevelled. He patted my shoulder and sprinkled holy water over the bed and held up the crucifix and murmured a few words of a prayer.

And then we watched, the three of us, as the morning broke and the sun shone weakly through the window and my mother shuddered away, and the last sound she made was like no other sound I'd ever heard, a sigh, the stuff of her life released from between her lips.

The nurse pulled the curtains and left me alone for a few moments. I looked at my mother's eyes, frozen open as though everything she'd seen was still preserved there in the retina, trapped in the amber of her last second on the earth. My shoulders began to shake and water streamed down my face, and I closed my eyes and summoned her every moment, dredged up all the days of her being from the centre of my body. I cried her out of me until I was dry.

Har helped me sort out the funeral arrangements, the death notice in the paper, the local-radio announcement, the flowers, the Mass cards. I had no idea there were so many things to do. Har went into philosophical mode.

'All this stuff is for the benefit of the living,' he said, 'not the dead. It's to keep people busy so they don't have time to come apart. It's after the funeral you have to watch out for. That's when it'll hit you.'

He pressed a wad of notes into my hand. It was more money than I'd ever seen. He wouldn't brook any argument.

'Take it, son.'

The night of the removals, I stood in the chapel yard and accepted hushed condolences and shook the hand of anyone who wanted their hand shook. Dee Corboy appeared out of the crowd. It was strange to see her all in black. She hugged me and waved her hands in front of her face, banishing invisible tears.

'Sorry,' she said. 'I'm useless at these things.' She waited beside me until everyone had gone and then she took my arm.

'C'mon,' she said. 'I'll buy you a drink.'

She brought me round the corner to The Ginnet. It was no bigger than a snug. Instead of Ladies and Gents signs on the toilet it had old Greek or Roman male and female symbols.

'I like it here,' Dee said. 'It's quiet. Mostly teachers and the drama-society crowd.'

'Kilcody has a drama society?'

'I was thinking of joining. I always wanted to act.'

She brought me a whiskey and a glass of wine for herself.

'Your health, Mrs Corboy,' I said, raising my glass.

'You'll really have to start calling me Dee. I won't be Mrs Corboy for much longer.'

She held up her bare ring finger. I didn't know quite what to say, so I just said I was sorry.

'Don't be,' she said. 'I'm not. Me and Ollie got a flat here in the village. I'm going back to college.'

She took a gulp from her glass and

stretched her legs. She was wearing black boots that came to her knees. The heels were lethal.

'Any word — '

'Last night. I told him your mother was very sick. He was sad to hear it. Said he'd write. He's been run off his feet what with everything that's happened.'

The whiskey glass stalled halfway to my mouth.

'Everything that's happened?'

She surveyed the blank look on my face.

'You haven't heard? Of course you haven't. You've had enough on your mind. It was in today's *Sentinel*.'

She opened her handbag and removed a newspaper clipping and passed it to me.

Hip-Hop Star Collaborates with Local Youth

by Jason Davin, Staff Reporter

A 17-year-old local youth became the talk of the domestic music industry this week when it was revealed that he has contributed lyrics to the forthcoming album by multi-platinum-selling hip-hop act Cujo aka Lewis Dillon.

James Corboy, formerly a resident of Fairview Crescent, Ballo town, became friends with the 22-year-old Brooklyn-born rapper when they met in Morocco last year. The two subsequently collaborated on some half-a-dozen songs for the as yet untitled new album. Industry sources have speculated that the teenager's lyrical input is likely to net him a substantial sum in royalties.

However, in a bizarre turn of events, it transpires that local Gardai are anxious to determine the current whereabouts of the youth, who allegedly absconded from Balinbagin Boys' Home last August, where he was serving a year on remand for charges relating to a burglary incident in Kilcody chapel last year. When contacted by the *Sentinel*, the youth's mother, Deirdre Corboy, declined to comment.

I placed the clipping back on the table.
'Is this a hoax?' I said.
Dee shook her head.
'The record company contacted me. I have to sign loads of papers because of his age. Apparently there's uproar around the village. Can you believe it?'
'I can,' I said, and smiled.
I handed Dee the clipping, but she waved it away.

'Keep it,' she said. 'I bought about ten copies to send to his aunts and uncles. God, I didn't even know he could write songs. I'm jealous.'

She took a sip of her wine.

'It's funny, he's only been gone a few months and I've almost forgotten what he looks like. I have to dig out old photographs to remember. Isn't that awful?'

I knocked back the whiskey.

'The same thing happened to me.'

We sat in silence. Dee looked at her watch.

'Oh dear. I have to pick up Ollie from his father's.'

She drained her glass.

'Walk me to my car.'

It wasn't exactly an order, but I got the feeling Dee was used to getting her own way. I guessed she was quite the princess when she was younger. Probably still was. Her new car was parked in the square.

'I made Maurice buy me that the week before I left him,' she said, neutralising the alarm with her zapper. 'Might trade it in though. I'm not used to an automatic. I don't know what to do with my hands.'

She gave me a squeeze.

'Don't stay out too late. You've a funeral to go to tomorrow.'

I watched her drive off and went back inside The Ginnet and sat at the bar, but no matter how many drinks I threw down my throat, I couldn't seem to get drunk.

The next morning I woke early and forced myself to wash and dress in the cleanest clothes I could find. The radio was forecasting storms, but still the weather held. There was a huge turn-out at the funeral. I did what was expected: walked behind the hearse and shouldered the coffin with Har and a few pallbearers from the funeral home. We set it down on slats placed over the open grave, gaping like a wound in the raw earth.

As the priest began to say the final words, Har slipped a hip flask of whiskey into my pocket.

'Medicinal purposes,' he muttered.

I took a swig on the sly and wondered where on earth Jamey was. At that moment, his absence was more acute than ever. I looked around at all the downcast faces.

'I didn't know she knew so many people.'

Har chuckled.

'She used to clean every house in Kilcody. These people told your mother things they wouldn't tell a priest.'

The breeze whispered through the leaves of the evergreens surrounding the graveyard. The priest finished with the prayers. We grabbed the straps and a couple of the men pulled away the boards. We lowered the coffin. When the pine box was settled in the pit and the straps had been retracted, I picked up a white wreath someone had placed at my feet and threw it into the open grave. As the first spade of dirt dissipated on the lid of the casket, I said goodbye, my mother among the flowers.

But it is written in the dream that at the end of time, the crows will regain their voices, and will praise their god, and sing.

11

Blowhole Cove felt like world's end, the last mapped part of the atlas, beyond which the sea might evaporate revealing monsters beached in the shallows, big-bellied mutations, lugworms the size of tree trunks.

Surf roared in my ears. The sky grumbled thunder, silencing the gulls. I gazed out across the sloblands and took a slug of whiskey from Har's hip flask, so bone-weary I feared I'd faint. The light had a brittle quality that made the eyeballs ache; fingers of blue electricity played about the glinting, flinty stones scattered on the strand.

Hours had passed since the funeral. I couldn't face an empty house so I took the road out of town, following my nose seaward, lulled into a sort of sleepwalk by the tattoo of my boots on tarmac. I just kept going until my feet ran out of land, by which time I was good and drunk.

I crested the hill and stumbled down the sandy slope to the water's edge. I stumbled over jellyfish slither and dead seaweed, following the shoreline through spits of rain and clouds of midges, and the fine white sand turned to mudflats strewn with rotten kelp. Combers foamed at the shore. That big old sea-hag bared her gums at me. The wind rippled my shirt and made panpipe sounds in the hip flask.

I pushed on, falling forward into my footsteps, until finally I rounded the curve of the coastline and came upon the inlet.

Sheltered from the wind and rain, I huddled in the mouth of Blowhole Cave and sipped whiskey. My chest was tight with phlegm and my ribcage ached and I realised that for the first time in days I was hungry, starving, digestive glands like thousands of hungry mouths.

Raindrops began to mottle the sand. I pulled my coat tight and watched as the sky darkened and the drizzle intensified until the sand ran like wounds. Lightning flared and thunderclaps rumbled like kettledrums across the jagged lower jaw of the horizon. The rain became a deluge, but inside the cave was dry. The blowhole sang, and in its keening I thought I could discern strains of the old hymn, my mother's lullaby.

Who's that a-writin'?

I curled up on the sand and closed my eyes and buried my head in the crook of my arm like a tired bird. And I passed out, out of myself and into the bottomless fall of sleep, my body sinking like a stone in murky water, falling until I opened my eyes and realised I wasn't falling at all, but lying spreadeagled on the sandy floor of some silent dream, staring at the inevitable sky.

And I saw him, winging towards me across the sea.

The old crow.

He glowed, huge and luminescent, moving over the waves, casting a vast galleon shadow on the sea. He drew closer still, wings beating, then hovered in a holding position and glowered and his head eclipsed the setting sun; he brought the night down with his wings and set his claws upon the sand, and whiteness spread all over his body, spread until every last feather gleamed. Then he took wing again, his great beak pointed toward the mountains.

Into the crags' jagged shadows he soared, over barren steppes of limestone stubbled with scutch unfit for goats, where the hill-fields reared up like great green-backed krakens, up, up, up he flew through the altitudes where the stratosphere darkened from pale blue to ink-dark, and foundling stars peeped through the sky like the faces of the dead, and his wings seemed to peel the heavens back, exposing a new heaven and a new earth beneath. The black sky cracked, hatching the sun; light dopplered out towards eternity as it crowned through the waters of the sound.

The storm had subsided. Scattered around me, streels of seaweed, bits of driftwood, jellyfish, crabs, gunk the sea chucked up.

The tide was coming in.

I got to my feet.

Above in the sudden blueness, gulls wheeled and whirled, and the sound they made was like bowed wood-saws, and their feathers were many-coloured. The sea was made of sky, the sky of sea.

Someone spoke my name. I turned and saw her walking towards me across the strand, and I stared, amazed at her face, her body restored to its fullness, her dress billowing in the wind, a single braid whipping about her shoulders.

She unlaced her boots and stepped out of them and walked into the sea that was the sky, and the blueness pooled around her feet.

She waded further in until it rose to her waist, and her dress floated out in a water flower shape and rose up to her shoulders, her neck, and she went under, her hair spreading like a fan, and she was gone.